STRIKE ZONE

ALSO BY DEREK JETER

The Contract

Hit & Miss

Change Up

Fair Ball

Curveballl

Fast Break

Baseball Genius

Double Play

STRIKE ZONE

DEREK JETER

with Paul Mantell

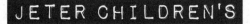

JETER CHILDREN'S

SIMON & SCHUSTER BOOKS FOR YOUNG READERS

New York   London   Toronto   Sydney   New Delhi

SIMON & SCHUSTER BOOKS FOR YOUNG READERS
An imprint of Simon & Schuster Children's Publishing Division
1230 Avenue of the Americas, New York, New York 10020

SIMON & SCHUSTER BOOKS FOR YOUNG READERS
is a trademark of Simon & Schuster, Inc.
For information about special discounts for bulk purchases, please
contact Simon & Schuster Special Sales at 1-866-506-1949 or
business@simonandschuster.com.
The Simon & Schuster Speakers Bureau can bring authors to your live event.
For more information or to book an event, contact the Simon & Schuster Speakers
Bureau at 1-866-248-3049 or visit our website at www.simonspeakers.com.
Book design by Krista Vossen
The text for this book was set in Centennial LT.
Manufactured in the United States of America
0320 FFG
First Edition
2 4 6 8 10 9 7 5 3 1
Library of Congress Cataloging-in-Publication Data
Names: Jeter, Derek, 1974- author. | Mantell, Paul, author.
Title: Strike zone / Derek Jeter ; with Paul Mantell.
Description: First edition. | New York : Simon & Schuster Books for Young Readers,
[2020] | Series: [The contract series ; 6] | Audience: Ages 8–12. | Audience: Grades
4–6. | Summary: Derek's season is not off to a good start, with his good friend on a
different team and his father unable to coach, and having a girl on his team only
complicates things more.
Identifiers: LCCN 2019031605 (print) | LCCN 2019031606 (eBook) |
ISBN 9781534454996 (hardback) | ISBN 9781534455016 (eBook)
Subjects: LCSH: Jeter, Derek, 1974– —Childhood and youth—Juvenile fiction. |
CYAC: Jeter, Derek, 1974– —Childhood and youth—Fiction. | Friendship—Fiction.
| Baseball—Fiction. | Sex role—Fiction.
Classification: LCC PZ7.J55319 Str 2020 (print) | LCC PZ7.J55319 (eBook)
DDC [Fic]—dc23
LC record available at https://lccn.loc.gov/2019031605
LC ebook record available at https://lccn.loc.gov/2019031606

To those I'm fortunate enough to call friends:
Thank you for the support, advice, and
encouragement.
—D. J.

A Note About the Text

The rules of Little League followed in this book are the rules of the present day. There are six innings in each game. Every player on a Little League baseball team must play at least two innings of every game in the field and have at least one at bat. In any given contest, there is a limit on the number of pitches a pitcher can throw, in accordance with age. Pitchers who are eight years old are allowed a maximum of fifty pitches in a game, pitchers who are nine or ten years old are allowed seventy-five pitches per game, and pitchers who are eleven or twelve years old are allowed eighty-five pitches.

Dear Reader,

Strike Zone is inspired by some of my experiences growing up. The book portrays the values my parents instilled in me and the lessons they have taught me about how to remain true to myself and embrace the unique differences in everyone around me.

Strike Zone is based on the life lesson that having a strong supporting cast is essential to success. On a team, just like in life, you need to surround yourself with supportive people with positive attitudes, strong work ethics, and qualities you value. This is one of the principles I have lived by in order to achieve my dreams. I hope you enjoy reading!

Derek Jeter

DEREK JETER'S 10 LIFE LESSONS

1. Set Your Goals High (*The Contract*)

2. Think Before You Act (*Hit & Miss*)

3. Deal with Growing Pains (*Change Up*)

4. The World Isn't Always Fair (*Fair Ball*)

5. Find the Right Role Models (*Curveball*)

6. Don't Be Afraid to Fail (*Fast Break*)

7. **Have a Strong Supporting Cast** (*Strike Zone*)

8. Be Serious but Have Fun

9. Be a Leader, Follow the Leader

10. Life Is a Daily Challenge

CONTRACT FOR DEREK JETER

1. Family Comes First. Attend our nightly dinner.
2. Be a Role Model for Sharlee. (She looks to you to model good behavior.)
3. Do Your Schoolwork and Maintain Good Grades (As or Bs).
4. Bedtime. Lights out at nine p.m. on school nights.
5. Do Your Chores. Take out the garbage, clean your room on weekends, and help with the dishes.
6. Respect Others. Be a good friend, classmate, and teammate. Listen to your teachers, coaches, and other adults.
7. Respect Yourself. Take good care of your body and your mind. Avoid alcohol and drugs. Surround yourself with positive friends with strong values.
8. Work Hard. You owe it to yourself and those around you to give your all. Do your best in everything that you do.
9. Think Before You Act.

Failure to comply will result in the loss of playing sports and hanging out with friends. Extra-special rewards include attending a Major League Baseball game, choosing a location for dinner, and selecting another event of your choice.

CONTENTS

STRIKE ZONE

Chapter One
CHANGE OF PLANS

"Go, Derek!"

As Derek Jeter went in for the layup, going airborne at full speed, the defender's arm came crashing down, slamming into Derek's ear and shoulder, making him cry out in pain.

But Derek had seen him coming. A split second before contact, he'd slipped the ball under and around the defender's crashing arm. A flick of Derek's wrist sent the ball spinning off the backboard, ricocheting back down and through the net, just as the ref's whistle blew! "And one!" Dave Hennum shouted from center court. Derek's best friend and teammate pumped his fist, then immediately ran to his side. "You okay?"

Derek was bent forward, one hand on his knee and the

other on his sore ear. "That hurt," he said with a grimace, then straightened up and rolled his shoulder around once or twice in its socket.

Then, turning to the ref, he put his hands up, asking for . . . the ball. Dave clapped him on the back. "That-a-way," he said. "Hit this shot, and we've got the game!"

Derek blew out a breath and tried to shake off the cob-webs from the blow he'd just taken. He knew that if he sank this free throw, his team, the Saint Augustine Friars, would be up by one point with only six seconds left. On the other hand, if he missed . . .

Derek focused on the rim, blowing out a long breath to calm his pounding heart. The hammer blow to his shoul-der hadn't helped any. Plus, his ear was still ringing.

It took all the concentration he could muster. But he had prepared himself for this moment all season long, as he rode the bench waiting for his chance to get in games. He'd dreamed of the time when he could show what he was made of when the critical moments came. Not just his talent, but his dedication to winning.

He blew out another breath, then readied his shot. Just as he was about to let it go, the ref's whistle blew again. "Time out, Green!" he shouted, pointing to the other team's coach.

Dave shook his head and frowned. "They're trying to ice you, Derek," he said. "Don't let it get to you."

Derek nodded, and they both headed to the bench,

where Coach Nelson already had the team gathered in a circle. "Okay, soon as the shot drops, everyone drop back to half-court and pick up your man there. Watch out for screens. And whatever you do—no fouls!"

Derek strode back to the line as the whistle blew for the resumption of play. He took the ball from the ref, bounced it three times, looked up at the basket, and without allowing a single thought to enter his head, threw it up. . . .

Swish!

In an instant, he was back in game mode, streaking toward half-court to join his teammates on defense. He turned just in time to see the inbound pass, a long lob, going over his head!

Derek stopped himself an instant before running into his man. Lucky thing, because a foul now could be disastrous!

Derek waved his hands wildly and moved his feet, making it hard for his man to get rid of the ball. Meanwhile, the clock was winding down. With only one second left, his man spun around, leaped, and tried to get off a last-second, game-winning shot.

Derek was ready for him. He'd known that if enough time ran off the clock, his man would have to take the desperation shot. Derek leaped right with him, and swatted the ball away!

Game over!

The Friars all ran onto the court and high-fived one another. It was a big victory, because it was the last game of the year, and now they'd finished their season with a winning record.

"Great job, Derek!" said the coach, giving him a slap on the back. "Oh. Sorry," he added as Derek winced. The coach had hit the same spot where Derek had just been slammed.

"Don't worry about it, Coach. It didn't hurt a bit," Derek answered with a grin.

He hugged Dave and his other teammates, shook hands with the losing team, and waved to his parents and sister, Sharlee, who were in the stands, cheering along with the rest of the home fans.

"Game ball to you, Jeter!" Coach Nelson said, handing it to Derek. Then he took out a Sharpie and signed it. "Next year, I've got a spot on the roster reserved for you, kid. See you at tryouts, huh?"

"*Yesss!*" Derek shouted, pumping his fist. "Thanks, Coach!"

"You earned it, kid," the coach said. "You came a long way your first season. It's not easy to ride the bench most of the year, cheer your teammates on, and be ready when your name is called. Even the best team needs its supporting players, not just stars. So hats off to you."

• • •

As the players emptied out their lockers for the season, Derek and Dave sat next to each other, stuffing their gym bags. "Wow," Dave said, shaking his head. "I can't believe the season is already over."

Derek laughed as he stared at the game ball. "I don't know. Seemed like a long season to me."

Dave understood. He'd played a lot while his friend sat on the bench. Dave was the third-tallest kid on the team, and played power forward.

"Anyway, it's over now. Time to look ahead," said Derek.

"I know what you're thinking," Dave said with a grin. "It's almost baseball season."

"That's right. Time to tee 'em up and let 'em fly!"

"Tee 'em up? That's funny."

Golf was Dave's passion, and Derek knew it. But Dave liked baseball, too. They'd been on the same team two years in a row. And last year, they'd been league champions— partly because Derek's dad and Dave's family's driver and helper, Chase Bradway, had been their coaches.

Derek was hungry for a repeat. "Envelopes went out yesterday, I heard," he said. "Call me as soon as you know, okay?"

"You too!"

If they were on the same team, with the same coaches— even if all the rest of their teammates were new—they'd have a great chance to repeat as champions!

Derek could already see it in his head . . . he and his

dad, Dave and Chase, and Derek's other best friend, Vijay, too—all holding up the trophy together. . . .

"The Yankees!" Derek shouted. "I'm on the Yankees! YESSS!"

Finally—after three years in Little League, and two years of T-ball before that! FINALLY, he was on the team of his dreams—the team he was aiming to play for someday in the big leagues! The Yankees!

Surely, it was a sign that this was going to be a very special season.

And if that wasn't enough of a sign, the phone rang twenty minutes later, and it was Vijay on the line. "Guess what?" he told Derek. "I'm on the Yankees!"

"ME TOO!" Derek yelled into the phone. "Woo-hoo!"

They'd been best friends ever since Vijay's family moved to Mount Royal Townhouses from India, way back when Derek was little. Not only that, they were almost always in the same class at school, and *always* on the same baseball team!

Derek knew he shouldn't get ahead of himself. But he couldn't help thinking about the fantastic season that was about to start!

He let himself get lost in daydreams . . . and then his dad came down for breakfast.

"Dad! Guess what? I'm on the Yankees! Finally!" "Well, that's great, son," said Mr. Jeter. "I know you've wanted that for a long time."

"We're going to win again, Dad!"

"Well, I'm sure you're going to try. You give it your best, and let's see how it all shakes out."

Something about the way he said it sounded wrong to Derek. *You*? Not *we*?

"Speaking of congratulations," said Mr. Jeter, "I have some really great news. I got promoted at work! I'm now *senior* counselor, thank you very much."

"Wow, that's great, Dad—congratulations! And did Mom hear anything about *her*—"

"Not yet, Derek," his dad cut him off, his smile fading. "Your mom hasn't heard anything, so let's give it a little more time before bringing it up. She'll mention something if there's anything to share."

"Okay, Dad, I won't."

Derek's sister, Sharlee, came bounding down the stairs. "Daddy! Derek!" she yelled. "How do you like my hat?" She was wearing a brand-new, bright yellow baseball cap with a T on the front. "See, Derek? I'm on the Lions! GRRR! Watch out—we bite!"

"That looks good on you," said Mr. Jeter. "Here, let me fix that brim for you. . . ."

"NO! Don't bend it, Daddy!" Sharlee said. "I like it this way."

"Okay, Sharlee," said her father. "You wear it however you want to. But Derek and I, we bend the front, old-school style."

Sharlee turned to Derek. "And with Daddy coaching my team, we're going to win, just like you did last year!"

"I guess we're both going to win, then," Derek said.

Mr. Jeter cleared his throat. "Let's talk about that. Derek, with this new promotion, I'll have to put in a few extra hours a week. I'm afraid that means I can only coach one of your teams this season, not both."

"Wait—you mean . . . ?"

"You remember last year, at the end of the season, I promised Sharlee I'd coach her team next season?"

"But I thought—"

"So did I, Derek," said his father. "Look, I'll still be able to come to some of the games, and offer any help I can, but—"

"Dad! *You can't not coach me!* What about—?" Derek fell silent. There was no "what about." Suddenly, all his lofty dreams came crashing back down to Earth.

"Don't worry, son. You've learned an awful lot these past few years, and you're getting better every season. Don't let this get in the way of all that progress. Besides, any games I can't make, your mom will attend."

Derek shook his head in disbelief. But what could he say? What could he do? He'd been rooting for his dad to get that promotion for the past two months, and now, it had come through. He knew he should be happy about it—and he *was*, kind of. But he also knew how important his dad's coaching had been to the team last year.

But wait, he thought—*there's still Chase!* He'd been a really good coach too. Maybe not as good as Derek's dad, but close enough. With him in charge, the team would still stand a great chance!

Then it hit him—*Dave hasn't called yet.*

Unable to contain himself, he picked up the phone and punched in his friend's number.

"Hey," said Dave. "I was about to call you—just opened my envelope."

"You'd better be on the Yankees," Derek said anxiously.

"Nuh-uh," Dave said, sounding disappointed. "Tigers."

"Tigers?" It was the team they'd both been on last season! "There must be a mistake," Derek said.

"I'm on the same team," Dave said. "What happened with you?"

"I don't know. But Vij is on the Yankees too."

"What? This is no fair!" Dave moaned. "We won the championship last year! Don't they have to give us a chance to repeat?"

"I guess not."

"Can't we complain or something?"

"I'm pretty sure it was done on purpose," Derek said. "They probably don't like it when the same kids win every year."

"Didn't your dad request us?"

"My dad's not coaching this season. He's coaching Sharlee's softball team instead."

"Oh man!" Dave moaned. "How come?"

Derek explained to Dave about his dad's promotion. "He was a really great coach too," Dave said sadly.

Suddenly, Derek realized something else. "Wait—is . . . Chase going to be coaching your team?"

"Yeah. I guess that's something, at least," Dave allowed. "But it really stinks for you and Vijay."

"Yeah," Derek said. "Tell me about it."

All his plans for the season had vanished into thin air. He would have to adjust to two new coaches and a whole new team—one without Dave, without Chase, and worst of all, without his dad.

Chapter Two

THE OTHER TWO SHOES DROP

"Look at the bright side," Vijay said as he and Derek tossed the baseball back and forth at the foot of Jeter's Hill. It was a sloping grassy area in the center of Mount Royal Townhouses where the local boys gathered to play ball whenever the weather and schoolwork allowed. The other kids called it Jeter's Hill because he was almost always there.

"Man, Vijay, don't you ever get down about anything?" Derek wondered.

"Research has shown that optimists are right eighty percent of the time," Vijay said with an emphatic nod of his head. "That's me. An optimist."

Derek shook his head, but he couldn't help smiling.

He knew Vijay had probably looked up the statistics—he always seemed to know his numbers, and never got less than an A-minus in math or science.

Even if the team finished dead last, Derek thought, at least Vijay would be there, finding whatever there was to feel good about, and making him feel better too.

"Hey, you guys! Over here!" Harry Hicks was coming toward them, riding his skateboard down one of the concrete paths that crisscrossed the grounds of Mount Royal Townhouses. He was wearing his baseball mitt, holding it up so they could throw him the ball while he was still in motion.

Derek tossed it his way, giving him just enough lead, and Harry made a circus catch, all the while trying not to fall off his board.

"Nice!" Vijay shouted, clapping.

"All day long," Harry said with a grin as he hopped off and came jogging over to join them. "Hey, what team you guys on?"

"Yankees," said Derek, without much enthusiasm.

"Me too!" Vijay said.

"Hey, me three!" Harry said jubilantly.

"All right!" Vijay said, high-fiving Harry.

Derek high-fived him too—but not quite so happily. Harry was a good ballplayer, sure. He could pitch and was a pretty decent hitter—but he came with a lot of attitude, and sometimes it was on the negative side.

Derek still remembered the time they'd all had to write essays about what they wanted to be when they grew up. Derek had written about someday being the starting shortstop for the New York Yankees. Harry had laughed in his face and told him to get real.

It was something that hurt Derek at the time. And still, all these years later, remembering Harry's words still carried a sting—even though Derek hadn't given up on his dream.

"Hey, is your dad coaching?" Harry asked him.

"Nah, not this year."

"Aw man," Harry groaned.

"You hear about anybody else?" Derek asked him.

"I hear Pete Kozlowski's on the team," Harry said. "And since your dad's not coaching, that means his dad's probably our coach."

Hearing this did not make Derek happy. Even though Pete was a big hitter with a lot of power in his bat, he and Derek had been teammates before—and it had not gone well. Pete had been a true problem child—selfish, and not at all a team player.

Worse, his dad, who'd been their coach, had let his son get away with it until very late in the season, when finally he'd had enough, and made Pete take a seat on the bench for a while.

Pete toned it down after that, and the team made the playoffs. But it had not been an easy time for

Derek—especially since Pete was a shortstop, just like him.

"How about your friend Dave?" Harry asked. "He on the team?"

Derek shook his head. "Tigers," he said.

"Bummer. He's a good hitter."

"Yup."

"On the other hand," Harry said, "look at the bright side. We've got me!"

"And Derek!" Vijay chimed in.

Great, thought Derek. Two *optimists*.

And then there was him.

Derek looked around at his teammates. There was Harry, on the mound. There was Vijay in center. And Pete, at shortstop.

Wait . . .

That couldn't be right.

If Pete was where he should be, where was Derek?

Now he saw that Pete was actually at first. And Harry was at second. And Pete was at third. . . .

Wait. How was that even possible?

"Derek!"

Derek snapped to attention—back in the classroom. Back in his seat, at his desk, surrounded by his classmates—every one of whom was now giggling at him, having a good laugh at his expense.

"Let me repeat myself, class," said Ms. Terrapin. "For the benefit of those of you with more important things to think about than science."

She looked right at Derek when she said it, and more giggles rippled through the room. "Your science projects this semester will count for twenty-five percent of your grade—that's one fourth, for anyone who might have been daydreaming when we covered fractions."

Another big laugh. "To make sure none of you lose focus," she went on, "I am going to pair each of you up with a teammate. You'll be graded as a team. I expect you to come up with an interesting project that your class-mates can learn from. You'll have to document your work, and present it to the class. You will have till May tenth. That gives you almost a month to complete your work. Now, let's begin."

She began to pair them up. Derek winced when Vijay was paired up with Sheila Lowe, who was class presi-dent. Sheila was also famous for having done all the dec-orations for last fall's talent show. Combined with Vijay's head for science (he wanted to be a doctor someday, just like his parents), those two would get an A-plus for sure, thought Derek.

Two by two, the students were teamed up. Derek watched as the available partners dwindled down to him and just a few others . . . including—*no, please, not him!*—Gary Parnell, Derek's nemesis.

"Darla, you work with Eugene . . . Marissa, you and Edward are a team . . . and, let's see—I guess that leaves you and Gary, Derek. There. That's done."

Nooooo!!!

Gary was staring at Derek from two rows away, a smug look on his face. Leaning in, he said in a low voice, "Don't worry, Jeter. You lucked out big-time. I've got this thing in the bag. We're gonna blow people's minds. No, wait—*I'm* gonna blow their minds, and *you're* gonna get a free A-plus."

"Wait a minute, Gary. I'm going to be doing half this project, so we're both going to earn the A-plus."

"Hmm. We'll see about that."

Derek shook his head in frustration. Gary was the smartest kid in the whole class, as he never got tired of reminding everyone. On the other hand—looking at the dark side—was an A-plus worth four weeks of torture?

Because working with Gary had the potential to be exactly that.

Chapter Three

OUT OF NOWHERE

Derek stared out the car window as he sat behind his mom, who was driving. Neither of them said much. He guessed she was thinking about the promotion at work she was waiting on.

Not knowing is hard, he thought. Just like it was for him, not knowing who was going to be on his team.

Vijay, seated next to Derek, was doing most of the talking. He seemed to be in a great mood, going on and on about spring being here, and what a beautiful day it was . . .

Well, it *was*.

Derek knew his friend had the right idea. Why should he upset himself in advance? Why should *anyone*?

There'd be plenty of time to be upset later, if things turned out badly.

Ugh. Now he felt even *worse.* Why was his stomach churning, anyway? He and Vijay had just had a snack before leaving.

"I'll be back at five to pick you up," Mrs. Jeter said as she dropped them off. "Sorry I can't stay the whole time, but I've got to go down to the office and drop off some work. Have fun."

"We will!" Vijay told her.

"Bye, Mom, see you later," said Derek, a little less excitedly.

He spotted Pete Kozlowski first thing—big, tall, with his dad right behind him, carrying the duffel bag with the team bats and helmets. Derek shook his head. Pete should have been helping, but he wasn't. Not a good sign, since Derek was hoping he'd changed his routine.

"Over there." Derek pointed, and he and Vijay made for the field where Pete and his dad were unloading.

There were four fields at Westwood, and they all met in the deep outfield. Hitting a ball so far it went onto someone else's field was something to brag about—and Pete had done it a couple times that Derek remembered.

There were three other kids there already. Two of them Derek recognized right away—and winced—Elliott Koppel and Norman Nelson. He remembered them from that same Tigers team, the one with Pete and his dad.

Elliott and Norman had been more interested in goofing around than in seriously playing the game. They always had a good time, but they sure didn't make the team any better. In fact, they'd badly sapped team spirit. But in the last game of the season, one of them—Derek forgot which—had made a spectacular play that won them the game.

So at least there was that.

Derek wondered if Norman could possibly be related to Mr. Nelson, Saint Augustine's hard-driving basketball coach.

No, there was no way that could be possible, he decided.

Either way, though, these Yankees were shaping up to be a bust so far.

The third kid standing with Norman and Elliott was Ryan McDonough, who had also been on that team. Ryan was a really good first baseman. He was twelve years old and already almost six feet tall. Derek could only imagine how much more power he had in his swing now that he had grown so much bigger.

Vijay greeted them all, and so did Derek—saving Pete for last.

"Jeter!" Pete said. "I knew you were gonna be here. Took a peek at my dad's roster last night."

"Same old Pete, huh?" Derek said, shaking his head.

"Why mess with success?" Pete shot back.

Derek nodded. "Hmm. Well, you're a lot bigger than last time I saw you."

"I grew six inches. Not you, though, I notice," Pete said,

giving Derek the once-over. "Still waiting on that growth spurt?"

Derek wanted to react, but just then, Mr. Kozlowski came over to say hello. "Hey! Derek! Great to see you, kid. You too, Vidgee!"

"It's Vijay," Vijay corrected him.

"Right. Right. I'll get it. Give me a little time. Good to see you guys again!"

"You too, Coach!" Vijay said cheerfully.

Harry arrived, and after him, two more kids who had been part of Derek and Vijay's championship team last year—Mason Adams and Miles Kaufman. Derek was glad to see Mason in particular. He was a speedy leadoff-type hitter and a real pest on the bases, plus he could play either second base or center field.

Miles was a good teammate, but not much of a hitter or fielder. On the other hand, he'd improved a lot with Derek's dad and Chase as his coaches. At least he would come to play every single game and give it his all. Derek hoped both he and Mason still remembered some of the coaching lessons they'd learned.

Other kids arrived—kids Derek didn't know, or at least not as baseball players. A couple went to Saint Augustine but weren't in his class. Two were from public schools in the area, and one from another private school. He sure hoped they were good players. If so, there was enough talent to make up a decent team. If not . . . well . . .

Finally, their other coach arrived with his son. At least this kid was carrying the duffel bag, Derek noticed.

This coach had the roster in his hand, and was going over it carefully, while Pete's dad looked over his shoulder, pointing out which kid corresponded to which name on the list. The other coach checked them off, then looked around in confusion, as if there were still someone missing. He looked at his watch, then started chewing on his pencil and pacing back and forth.

Meanwhile, everyone else seemed to be trying to get his attention. All the boys were throwing balls back and forth to one another—grounders, pop-ups, liners, dribblers—trying to make every play look spectacular to impress the coaches.

Pete's dad was now focused on his own son. It was just the same as Derek remembered from three years ago.

"Atta boy, Pete! Great play, great play!" And Pete, tipping the brim of his cap like he was saluting the roaring crowd at Yankee Stadium. Derek shook his head slowly. Someone else might make a really great play, and Pete's dad would never even notice.

Derek did a quick head count. Twelve kids. Usually, teams had thirteen, so he understood why the coach kept looking around for the missing kid.

But it was getting late. They only had two hours here, and Derek wanted to get out on that field and see what the Yankees had going!

Finally, a kid in jeans and a baseball cap hopped out of

a car that had pulled up to the curb. The kid was headed straight for them, waving, and the coach was waving back. "Okay," he said with a big sigh. "Here we go."

As the kid approached, Derek got the sense that there was something different about him. And then, suddenly, he knew what it was—*the kid was a girl!*

She removed her cap, and long brown hair tumbled out. "Sorry I'm late, Coach," she said.

Every other kid on the team stared, open-mouthed. "Okay," the coach answered in a surprisingly forgiving tone. "From now on, everyone gets here on time, all right? You all hear that?"

Some kids mumbled "Yes, Coach," but most were still just staring at the new arrival.

A girl! Derek thought, alarmed. *And she's on my team! How are we ever going to win now? Or even make the playoffs?*

The other kids started glancing at one another, and Derek heard a few uneasy murmurs, then a tense giggle or two.

He looked back at the girl. If she heard the noise, she was doing a good job of ignoring it—concentrating instead on breaking in her mitt, grinding a ball into it and squeezing it shut with both hands. Then she adjusted her cleats, which, like her mitt, were brand-new.

Finally, the coach spoke up and broke the awkward near-silence. "Okay, gather around, everyone. Let me call the roll."

He began calling out the names. Derek called "here" when his was called. Then he waited to hear the girl's name.

"Avery Mullins?"

"Here," she said.

Avery. Derek had known a *boy* back in kindergarten with that name. So maybe the coach hadn't known in advance that he had a girl on his roster.

Or maybe he *had*. He'd sure looked nervous waiting for her to show up.

Derek wondered if her parents were in the stands. He couldn't tell. But then the girl looked over there and waved—and two guys in their teens waved back. Her brothers? Derek had no idea, but he didn't see anybody else waving.

"Okay. I'm Coach Jay Stafford. Some of you know my son JJ. . . ." The coach's son, a kid Derek didn't know at all, held up his hands as if to say, *No applause, please.*

"And this is Mr. Kozlowski. He'll be my assistant."

"Call me Coach K," said Pete's dad.

"I've coached a few of you before, but most of you are new to me," Coach Stafford resumed. "So, let me see, by a show of hands—how many of you have played Little League ball before?"

A sea of hands went up. In fact, there was only one kid whose hand remained down—Avery Mullins.

All eyes swung to her. Derek could see that her cheeks were red with embarrassment. She sat there, staring at the ground, until the coach continued his speech.

"All right, that's no problem," he said cheerily, clapping his hands together. "You'll get the hang of it, kid—I mean, we all have to start somewhere."

Soft groans went up all around Derek. The coach ignored them.

"Okay, are you guys ready to show me and Coach K what you can do out there?"

"YEAH!" everybody shouted.

It was the first real enthusiasm all day.

Derek noticed that his coaches acted as if everything was *normal*—as if this was just a normal team having a normal practice.

Only there was nothing normal about any of it.

Most girls he knew played softball—*with other girls.* Nothing wrong with that. Derek liked a good game of softball himself. In fact, he knew a few girls who could throw a softball faster than he could throw a baseball.

His grandma had told him that years back, a law was passed that said girls were allowed to play sports on any team they qualified for—even boys' teams.

But he had never met a girl who *actually played* baseball. Until now.

If the Yankees were the only team in the whole league with a girl on its roster, it wasn't really fair, Derek thought. How were they supposed to compete with teams that didn't have any?

Chapter Four
REELING AND DEALING

"Okay," Coach Stafford said, "let's form up two groups—one with me, and one with Coach K."

Derek went to Coach Stafford's side—he never had warmed up to Coach Kozlowski much. Vijay, naturally, went with him, as did Harry, Mason—and Avery.

Pete, of course, was in his dad's group. They took positions out in the field, so that Pete's dad could hit them some balls. Derek's group, meanwhile, was positioned to run the bases, while Coach Stafford timed them with a stopwatch, writing down their times in his roster book for future reference.

Mason had the fastest time in their group. No surprise there. Derek had never played with anyone who was faster going around the bases. There was no doubt in his mind that Mason would wind up leading off.

Derek thought for sure he would have the second-fastest time going from home to first. He'd pretty much led his team in stolen bases every year—except last year, when Mason was his teammate. But to his surprise, Derek wound up placing third—beaten out by a girl, no less!

Not only was he surprised, but he was annoyed as well. He didn't like being beaten out by *anybody*! As they lined up again, this time to run all the way around the bases, Derek was determined to salvage his honor.

Avery went before him. She sailed down the baseline to first in no time flat. But the path she took around the bases cost her time. When it was Derek's turn, he rounded the bases so efficiently that he beat her time by a full second.

There. That felt better.

The boys in the group kept whispering to one another, avoiding conversation with Avery. If she noticed, she did a good job of hiding it. Her attention stayed focused on the task at hand. She was as serious as an executioner. No smiles, no jokes—not a word out of her. Derek was impressed.

The two groups switched places and coaches. Derek trotted out to shortstop—and so did two other boys. Avery positioned herself right behind second base—not where any player would be during a real game, but then again, this was just fielding practice, and all the other positions were taken by boys who were sure to hog any balls that came their way.

Coach Kozlowski started hitting balls to the different areas. "Take turns!" he called out, so that the boys wouldn't crash into one another trying to make a play.

Things went all right, until he hit a pop-up Avery's way.

"I got it! I got it!" shouted Harry, racing over from the right side.

"Me! Me!" Norman yelled, running in from left field.

Avery, who had been the obvious one to make the catch, ducked when she heard them coming her way. At the same time, both Norman and Harry pulled up for fear of running into each other. The ball fell right between them, two feet in front of Avery, and lay there on the infield dirt.

Harry grabbed it and threw it back in. "That was my ball," he muttered angrily.

"I had it!" the would-be shortstop shot back.

Neither one of them even looked at Avery, who was just standing there, glaring back at them.

Derek expected Coach Kozlowski to say something—*anything*. But he didn't. Nor did he hit another one to Avery but went on instead to the next position—Derek's.

Derek had no time to think about what had just happened. He had to make a play on the soft liner that was about to drop in front of him. He dove, snagging it just before the ball hit the ground.

"All right! Nice play!" Coach K said, pointing the bat at Derek. Derek wanted to smile, but fought it, pounded his glove and got into his ready stance, all business.

Coach K kept on hitting balls to the fielders. The next time he got around to Avery, he hit her a sharp grounder. She was getting into position to field it when Elliott, playing short right field, raced over and dove for the ball, knocking it out of Avery's reach.

"Gotta call it!" Coach K called, pointing to her. "That's your ball, gotta call it and go for it!"

Derek knew it hadn't been her fault. She'd been in position when the other kid came in and knocked it away. But Derek understood. The kid had just assumed that a girl would muff the play if he didn't go for it himself.

Derek wondered if she would have caught it—it was a pretty sharp grounder, well hit and right at her. She might have flinched. But they weren't going to find out now—not today, anyway.

Before it came around to Avery's turn again, they went on to another drill. This time, all the kids, from both groups, were asked to pair up and throw to each other.

Derek was immediately approached by Vijay, and the two of them started tossing it back and forth. But Derek noticed that Avery was just standing there, waiting for someone to partner with her.

Nobody did. She waited and waited, even after everyone else was paired up. Finally, Coach Stafford took notice, and said, "Here you go, kid—you and me." And they started tossing it back and forth.

Derek couldn't help thinking what it would be like to be in her shoes. Sure, she was a girl, and girls were different. Either way, though, it was no fun to be ignored and snubbed by everyone around you.

Avery, meanwhile, kept acting like nothing was wrong. She ignored the other kids right back and went about her business.

Pretty cool, Derek thought admiringly. She was tough, and focused—and fast, too, even though she needed to improve her baserunning. As he watched, Derek couldn't help observing that she could catch and throw as well as most of them.

"Hey! Heads up!" Vijay called. Derek stopped thinking about Avery's feelings. He didn't want to try *too* hard to put himself in her shoes. After all, what was she doing here in the first place?

The whole business could only hurt the team, he reasoned. Even if she wound up being a decent player, just her *being* there was bound to cause problems.

He wasn't just guessing about it, either. Derek was keeping his doubts to himself, but some of the other boys weren't being so polite.

"This stinks," he heard Pete say, loud enough for anyone nearby to hear.

"Totally," Harry agreed, throwing the ball back to Pete.

Derek didn't need to ask them what they meant. He could see them glancing Avery's way.

Elliott and Norman were busy cracking each other up with whispered comments and sidelong looks at Avery. Elliott even mimed throwing the ball "like a girl"—off the wrong foot.

Not that Avery threw like that. But it didn't matter to them. They were having a good old time.

For the last fifteen minutes of practice, each player got one turn at bat, while the rest rotated positions in the field. Coach K did the pitching himself, lobbing easy ones in there while Coach Stafford did the catching.

Derek hit a screaming liner over Pete's head at short-stop and legged out an easy double. "Nice going, Derek!" Coach K told him, pointing at him approvingly.

Derek was glad to be singled out like that. He'd improved a lot since the last time Coach K had seen him, and he was eager to show it off.

When it was her turn, Avery swung hard—right through the first two pitches. There were sniggers and hoots from a lot of the boys, although the two teenagers who had come with Avery cheered her on from the stands.

"She swings like a zombie," Derek heard Pete say.

"Like a droid," Harry corrected him.

Derek was sure Avery could hear them both. He saw her shoulders sag for an instant, as if she'd been hit with a hard object. But she recovered her focus and sent a fly ball to center. Miles ran it down pretty easily, but at least she'd hit it hard and far.

Derek knew it wasn't easy to hit while people were trying to psych you out. Not for the first time today, he found himself impressed by Avery's grit.

She'd managed to shake off her emotions in the batter's box. But Avery had a tougher time out in the field. Rotating positions along with the others, she found herself at second base when Vijay hit a sharp grounder her way.

As she got into position to make the play, Pete, at first, made a sudden sound—"HAH!" It rattled Avery enough that she bobbled the ball, allowing Vijay to reach base safely.

Pete just laughed. Harry, over at third, joined in, as did a few others. Not Derek or Vijay, though.

If either of the coaches had noticed any of this, they showed no sign of it.

Avery got another chance while at third. This time she fielded the ball, and was about to throw to first when Harry, at shortstop, yelled, "Here!"

She'd been about to fire to first, but Harry's shout made Avery freeze mid-throw. The ball dropped out of her hand and landed on the ground in front of her.

"Ohh! E-five!" Harry moaned mockingly, pretending to be the play-by-play announcer. E-five meant an error by the third baseman.

This time, Avery didn't ignore it. She stood there, glaring at Harry, leaving the ball right there on the ground.

"What?" he asked, pretending innocence.

Avery shook her head. "You weren't even covering a base," she said. "Why were you calling for the throw?"

"Whoa!" Harry said in exaggerated shock. "Ex-cuuuuse me!" That cracked a bunch of kids up.

"Okay, that's it for today!" Coach K called out and blew his whistle.

Derek watched as Avery shuffled slowly toward the stands. The two teenage boys were clapping for her, but she was staring at the ground and seemed not to notice. They patted her on the back and hugged her. Derek thought he saw her wipe a tear from her eye.

Or maybe it was just dirt. . . .

Derek felt like he should go over and say something to her. A compliment, or something encouraging. After all, even though they were stuck with a girl on the team, making her feel rotten wasn't going to help her play any better. More like the opposite. And how exactly was that supposed to help the Yankees win?

Derek started toward her, but as he got closer, he could feel the eyes of the other kids on him. If he said something to her, they'd all notice—and who knew what they would think or say?

So instead of talking to her, Derek turned and walked right past her, over to where Mason was standing.

"Hey, man," said Mason. "Good to have you on the team again."

"Yeah. You too." Glancing back at Avery, Derek caught her staring right at him. He quickly looked away, wondering if she'd read his mind.

He hoped not. Because that would definitely hurt her feelings even more. As bad as he felt about things, he knew that Avery had to be feeling much, much worse.

"And Daddy timed us all running around the bases? And I was the fastest one!"

Sharlee was practically bouncing up and down in her seat at the dinner table. "Daddy is the best coach in the whole wide world! And my team is *sooo* good—Ciara is on it too— and we're going to hit a bunch of homers, right, Daddy?"

"You're all going to do just fine," Mr. Jeter said with a hint of a smile. "You just keep working hard on your skills, like your brother."

"Derek," said Mrs. Jeter, who'd been quiet up till now, "is something bothering you?"

"Me?"

"You seem a thousand miles away—and not in a happy place."

Derek sighed. "I'm fine, Mom."

"Well then, don't look so down when your sister's telling you how well her day went."

"Do I have to be happy every single minute?"

"You don't—but don't rain on anyone else's parade," said his dad. "Everybody's feelings matter as much to them as yours do to you. And if you're not willing to talk about what's got you down, don't lay it on the rest of us and sit there frowning."

Derek sighed again. "Sorry. Sorry, Sharlee."

"That's okay, Derek," said his sister. "I accept your apology. And I'm sorry you can't have Daddy for your coach, like me."

Derek was about to roll his eyes—but stopped himself. He knew his parents were right, and that if Sharlee was happy with her day, he shouldn't try to bring her down just because *he* was upset.

Obviously, she thought his bad mood was all because of their dad coaching *her*, not *him*. But that wasn't even the half of it.

There was Pete and his dad. There was the girl. And on top of it all, there was Gary Parnell, who always seemed to find his way into Derek's nightmares.

After dinner, he helped his mom wash the dishes. The Jeters didn't have a dishwasher—there wasn't room for one in their small kitchen—but Derek didn't mind. In fact, he liked having this time with his mom. It was when they did some of their best talking.

"You sure you don't want to talk about it, old man?"

Old man. It's what she'd called him ever since he could remember. "Because you're wise beyond your years," his mom had told him.

"I don't know. It's a bunch of things. . . ."

"Like what? I'm listening."

"Like I got paired with Gary Parnell for our science project. I have to work with him on it for the next four weeks."

"Hmm." She washed a dish and handed it to Derek. "Well, look at the bright side—you'll probably get an A between the two of you." Derek's mom was familiar with Gary, since he and Derek had been in the same class every year at Saint Augustine's.

"A-plus," Derek agreed. "But it's going to be—"

"Uh-uh," Mrs. Jeter stopped him. "It's going to be whatever you make of it. If you decide in advance that it's going to be a bad experience, you'll surely make it happen. You might as well make the best of it, especially since you can't avoid it."

Derek wasn't totally sure about that last part. Avoiding it hadn't occurred to him till now, but since she'd brought it up . . .

"So . . . what else is bothering you?" she said, returning to the matter at hand.

"Dad not being my coach, Chase not being my coach, Dave not being on my team, Pete Kozlowski and his dad . . ."

"Okay, I get it. It's not the team you dreamed about being on," his mom said. "But Derek, it's *your* team. You've got to do whatever you can to help them win—not sit around and mope about things you can't change."

Derek nodded, staring at the plate he was drying. He knew she was right. But he still hadn't told her about the girl. . . .

"Anything else?" his mom asked.

Should he tell her? Part of him wanted to—but he figured she'd probably just say "make the best of it." He already knew that, so what was the point? Besides, his mom was a woman. How could he complain to her about having a girl on his team?

"No, that's it, I guess." He stared at the dish he was holding. "So, Mom, what about you? What's going on with that promotion? Are you getting it?"

He'd said it to get the focus off himself and onto her. But he knew right away that he'd goofed. His dad had warned him not to bring it up, and he'd totally forgotten! He wished he could take back his words, but it was too late now.

Sure enough, her expression darkened, and the sympathetic smile faded from her lips.

"No. I haven't heard anything. Not yet."

"Well," said Derek, trying to soften the edge of his words, "I guess these things take time."

She shook her head slowly, staring out the window over the sink, into the darkness outside. "I have a bad feeling about it," she said softly. Then she turned to him and smiled sadly. "I know, I know, I've just been telling you to look at the bright side and make the best of it. But it's taking too long, and no one is saying a word to me."

She turned away and looked out into the darkness again. "I'm trying to stay positive, believe me," she said. "But it's getting harder every day."

Derek felt bad for his mom. She didn't deserve that kind of treatment. Not from the company she'd worked so hard for, and for so long. Not from *anybody*!

Then he thought about the girl. *Avery*. He remembered her standing there, all during practice and afterward, all alone . . . no one saying a word to her . . .

Chapter Five
GETTING IN DEEPER

"Wait a minute! Where do you think *you're* going?"

Derek froze where he stood. Kids filed down the hall-way past him in both directions.

It wasn't the principal, or the dean, whose voice had made him stop in his tracks.

No. It was someone *much scarier*—Gary.

"Let me guess—you were trying to sneak out of here with-out having our meeting." Gary stared at Derek in disbelief.

"No, Gar, really," Derek said, not too convincingly. "I was just—"

"Don't give me that," Gary said, waving a hand dismis-sively. "You've been avoiding me ever since we got paired up on this assignment."

"I have not! It's just—"

"Just, nothing," Gary interrupted. "What were you thinking, Jeter? We've already lost a whole week because of you! Are you trying to sabotage us?"

"No!"

"To put it in terms you understand: We're a *team*. And you know who the *captain* of that team is, right?"

Derek heaved the book bag off his shoulder and dropped it to the ground. "Okay," he said. "You win. Where to?"

"Follow me."

Gary led him back down the hall and into the math lab. "It's quiet here," he said. "Chess club meets Mondays and Fridays, but it's dead otherwise."

Gary dropped his book bag onto one of the long desks that filled the empty classroom and pulled out a sheaf of papers and drawings. "Okay, Jeter. You ready to get to work?"

"What do you mean? We haven't even come up with an idea yet."

"*We?* What is this 'we' of which you speak? *I* have three ideas here for us to choose from."

"Oh! Great." Derek was genuinely surprised, and tentatively pleased.

"Well, I figured *you* wouldn't have any ideas, so . . ."

"Hey! What do you mean by that?"

"Have you *ever* had an original idea in your head, Jeter? Don't bother answering, we're short on time here."

"But—"

"Anyway, I'm way ahead of you, as usual. So here are my three ideas, each more brilliant than the one before."

Derek gritted his teeth to keep from exploding in frustration as Gary unfolded a large sheet of art paper. It had a drawing of a rocket of some kind. "It has to have an engine, of course," Gary said. "We'll have to build one. We'll also need a safe space to shoot it off."

And where are we going to get that? Derek wondered. "Brilliant, Gary," he said, trying to sound sarcastic.

But Gary just accepted the compliment as if it were his due. "Thank you. I'll admit it would be hard to pull off, but actually the engine would be the most fun part to build. Better than gluing together the frame and the ultralight cladding—"

"Next?"

Gary frowned. "Okay, okay." He unfolded another sheet with another drawing. "This one compares the environmental factors of a saltwater fish tank versus a freshwater fish tank."

"Uh . . . with fish?"

Gary looked at Derek as if he were from Mars.

"Jeter, are you all there? How are we going to do a fish experiment without fish?"

"But . . . do you have fish at home?"

"No. I've been asking my mom for years, but she always says no way." He looked up at Derek and smiled. "That part will be your job!" he said brightly.

"Wait a minute! Are you for real? I'm not going to ask my parents to put in two—not one, but two—fish tanks! I don't even *want* fish!"

"Well!" Gary sounded offended. "I sure hope you like idea number three, because we're going to do one of these."

"Says who?"

"Says *me*. Until you come up with an idea of your own, that's how it's going to be."

What could Derek say? He honestly hadn't given the project a single thought until now. They didn't have that much more time to waste coming up with an idea.

That being said, Gary's first two ideas were nonstarters. For one thing, they would take way too much time. And the last thing Derek wanted to do was spend lots of time with Gary.

"Idea number three—ta-da!" Gary proudly unfolded another large sheet of paper.

"It looks like a maze, kind of." Derek cocked his head one way, then the other, to try to decipher Gary's scribbling and crazy drawing style.

"It is! This project measures the ability of rats to learn, given different stimuli, like alcohol."

"*Rats?*" Derek repeated. "Gary, I have serious doubts my parents would let me bring rats into the house. Not to mention they're the creepiest animals ever."

"Well," Gary said, considering. "I suppose we could use mice instead."

"Sure," Derek said. "At *your* house, though."

Derek figured that would be the end of idea number three. But to his surprise, Gary said, "Okay. I'll run the experiments at my house—once you build the maze."

"*Me?* Build the maze—*by myself?* Wait a minute!"

"Come on, Jeter, we all know I'm the brains of this outfit, and you're the brawn."

"*I* don't know that," Derek protested, but Gary ignored him.

"Look, I'm agreeing to have the mice at my house, okay? I've given you exact specifications and measurements for the building of this maze. Surely you don't expect me to do *everything*."

"But *I'd* be doing all the work!"

"*Aww*. My heart bleeds for you! All you've got to do is build the maze, and do all the documentation of my experiments."

"Docu—"

"Well, of course! It's all got to be written up! You heard Ms. Terrapin."

"I'm doing *everything* here!"

"You shouldn't shout, Jeter," Gary said. "This is supposed to be a quiet space."

Derek suppressed the urge to knock over every chair in the room. He was caught, and he knew it.

"Besides, I've already done most of the hard work—coming up with a great idea. All that's left is to convince my mom to let me get the mice."

"She'll never do it," Derek said, spotting what he thought was a fatal flaw in Gary's plan. "She wouldn't even let you have *fish*—you said so yourself."

"Fish, and fish tanks, and fish equipment, are all expensive," Gary explained. "Once you've spent all that money, you kind of commit to a long-term project. But mice? In a maze you build and bring over to my house for a week or two?" He smiled. "Once the project is over, the maze goes in the garbage."

"And the mice?" Derek asked.

Gary shrugged. "Let 'em loose somewhere outside," he said matter-of-factly. "Maybe right outside your house, Jeter. Ha!"

Watching as Gary hooted with laughter and clapped his hands, enjoying his own sick joke, Derek wondered how he was ever going to get through three more weeks of this torture.

One thing was for sure—no matter how much positive thinking he did about it, working with Gary was going to be a monumental pain.

"Throw me a short hop," Derek told Vijay. Vijay did.

"Harder this time," Derek said. "Make it tough for me."

Vijay threw the ball as hard as he could. It landed just to Derek's left and a little in front of him. Derek reached across and backhanded the ball. Having grabbed it, he did a little crow hop and fired it back to Vijay.

"And he's out!" Vijay cried. "Yesss! Awesome pick by Jeter at short, and he just nips the runner!"

This was how things often went at Jeter's Hill on a typical spring day after school. Derek wasn't usually the first one there—his parents always made him finish his homework first—but he was here every day, rain or shine. Which was why the kids nicknamed it Jeter's Hill.

"Okay, now to my right side," Derek instructed. This time, Vijay fired the short-hop grounder too far wide, and Derek's leaping try for the grab came up empty.

Luckily Harry, a bat slung over his shoulder with his mitt hanging from the end of it, was right there to bend down and scoop up the errant throw.

"Gotta snag those, Jeter," he said, casually flipping the ball to Derek as he approached.

"Right," Derek said, cracking a smile. The boys on the hill were always ribbing one another, but it was all in good fun.

"You're late," Derek said. "Take the outfield."

"I'm a pitcher, not an outfielder," Harry shot back.

"Fair enough. And I'm an infielder." They looked at each other, then both of them looked at Vijay.

"Okay, okay, I'll take the outfield," Vijay said, laughing. "Just to keep the peace."

"Hey," Harry said as Vijay was about to head up the hill, past the bare patch in the grass that served as second base for their pickup games. "What are we gonna do about the girl?"

Vijay and Derek looked at each other. Then they looked at Harry. Then back at each other.

"I know, I know," Harry went on. "It really stinks that we got stuck with her."

"Wait a minute, Harry," Vijay said quickly, holding up a hand. "Maybe it will turn out to be a good thing. You never know."

Derek was glad Vijay had spoken up first. He himself would not have known what to say.

"'You never know'? *Of course* you know!" Harry shot back. "She's a *girl*, Vij! A girl playing a guys' game!"

"Who says it's just for guys?" Vijay said, shrugging. "Besides, she seems like a good enough player."

Harry squinted hard at Vijay. "What, do you *like* her or something?" he asked, shaking his head in confusion.

"No!" Vijay said quickly. "No—I am just saying, how do you know it will be a bad thing in the end?"

"Isn't it obvious?" Harry asked. "Derek—tell him."

Great, thought Derek. *Now I'm on the spot for sure.* "I don't know, Harry. She didn't look that awful out there."

"She messed up plenty," Harry said flatly. "You saw."

"No more than a lot of the other kids. And a bunch of times, other kids were trying to mess her up. None of us looked that great out there, honestly."

"Oh my gosh," Harry said, shaking his head disgustedly. "Don't tell me *you* like her *too*?"

"Cut it out, will you?" Derek said, getting annoyed. "I

didn't say I was *happy* about her being there."

"Are you?" Harry asked point-blank.

Derek shrugged, struggling to find the right words. "It's nothing personal against her," he said. "It's just . . ."

"I know!" Harry said, jumping in. "It's just *wrong*, is all. Just plain *wrong*."

Derek didn't argue with Harry. But *wrong* was not the word he was going to use. He'd been about to say that having a girl on the team was *hard to get used to*.

Chapter Six
AWKWARD MOMENTS

The Yankees' last practice before the season began was already in full swing. After twenty minutes of drills, Coach Stafford gathered the team together, and told them the rest of the day would be devoted to deciding player positions and the starting lineup for Saturday's game.

Everyone trotted out to their preferred positions to start the process. Derek was so fast getting out to short that for a brief moment, he was the only one there. He scanned the infield as the other kids followed. Then came Pete, straight toward him.

Well, that was no surprise. Ever since he discovered that both Pete and his dad were part of the Yankees,

Derek figured Pete would be competing with him for the shortstop spot, just like three years ago.

But as Pete reached the mound, he made a sudden turn and headed for second base instead. "Ha-ha!" he said, pointing at Derek. "Faked you out!"

Derek didn't mind Pete having a laugh at his expense—not if it meant he wasn't going to challenge him for shortstop! But he wondered why Pete had chosen not to. Maybe he'd decided being beaten out once was enough.

Derek shook his head. If the shoe had been on the other foot, he knew he wouldn't have backed down. He would have seen it as a challenge to take back the position he'd lost.

He looked around now to see where everyone else had planted themselves. Alongside him at short were two other kids: Elliott and a kid named Mark.

Fair enough, thought Derek. He was pretty confident he could hold his own against these two.

Derek saw that Harry and Tre', one of the kids who was new to Derek, were trying out at third. Ryan McDonough was at first, as was Miles.

And at second, along with Pete, was Avery. Pete kept giving her sidelong stares, as if to say *I can't believe this girl has the gall to try out for the infield!*

Avery paid no attention at all to Pete. She also ignored the muttering from some of the others who were talking behind their mitts, cracking one another up.

As far as Derek could make out, Avery didn't find

anything funny—least of all the fact everyone was making jokes about her. She was all business.

Like me, Derek couldn't help thinking.

Coach K began hitting grounders to the infield candidates. One to third, then to short—a hot smash to Derek's left that he dove, snagged, and fired to first, where Ryan grabbed it.

Then it was the second basemen's turn. Derek noticed that Coach K hit his son a nice, easy two-hopper. Pete handled it easily. *He could have done it with his eyes closed*, Derek thought.

After three turns around the field, Coach K called out "Switch!" Derek stepped back to let Elliott take his turn. Derek had made three tough plays and shown he could handle them perfectly. So far, so good.

Elliott bobbled the first chance he got at short. He threw it over Miles's head at first on the second. Derek felt better and better about his chances to be the starter at short.

Then Coach K hit one to Avery—a screaming short-hop grounder that ate her up completely.

She had no chance, Derek thought. *There isn't a kid on the team who would have made that play. Not even me, probably.*

On Avery's next chance, Coach K hit her a dribbler that she had to charge. She picked it up fine, but had to twist and throw off-balance to first, and wound up tossing it into the stands instead.

"Nice one!" Pete said, clapping his hand on his mitt. That sent Norman and Elliott into gales of laughter, and other boys into another round of whispered comments.

It was Vijay who ran to get the ball and toss it back in. Everyone else just stood there, waiting, staring at Avery—who was doing her best to pretend nothing was up.

Her third fielding chance was no less difficult. It was a high hop, deliberately hit that way by Coach K. Avery handled it and made a decent, quick toss to first, but it was low, and Ryan dropped it. "Safe!" yelled Pete, getting another laugh.

Derek found himself getting really angry. He didn't like the idea of having a girl on the team any better than they did—but he hated bullying and ganging up on kids worse. He knew that if Pete had been at second base for those three balls his father hit Avery, he would have muffed them too.

"Okay," Coach Stafford said when the fielding tryouts were done. "Now let's have you take turns hitting."

For the first round, Derek stayed at short, with Pete at second and Ryan at first. Looking around at who was playing the rest of the positions, Derek guessed that these would be the starting fielders for game one. The kids hitting now would probably be the subs.

Avery was one of them, he noticed. With Harry pitching to her, she took two vicious, healthy-looking swings, but came up empty on the first and fouled the second one off weakly.

"Hey, it's Babe Ruth!" Pete joked, loud enough for every-one to hear. "Go, Babe!"

"Hey!" Avery stepped out of the batter's box and pointed at Pete. "Quit calling me Babe."

"Ooh! I'm sooo scared!" Pete shot back, doubling over with laughter.

Derek had heard all he could stand. "Zip it, Pete," he said, glaring at him.

Pete's laughter came to a sudden stop. *"What did you just say?"*

"Just cut it out, okay?"

"Whooooaa." Pete slowly straightened up and looked Derek in the face. "So that's how it is, huh?"

"I don't know what you're talking about," Derek shot back. "Just play ball, okay?"

"Everybody back to your positions! Let's go! We don't have all day!" Coach Stafford shouted, clapping his hands.

Avery got back in the box, and Harry threw her a fast-ball. She hit it hard to short. Derek grabbed it just before it got past him and fired to first to beat her by a step.

"Nice play, shortstop!" called Coach Stafford. Derek nodded, then glanced over at Avery, who was walking back toward the plate staring at the ground. All eyes fol-lowed her every step.

Soon it was time for the groups to switch places. Avery went out to second base, and Pete came to the plate. Now it was Mason pitching instead of Harry, who was swinging a bat on deck.

Pete hit a hard grounder right past the mound. Elliott ran behind second to make the grab, then flicked it behind his back to Avery, who was covering second.

She made the catch, pivoted, and fired to first for the double play . . .

Except that her throw was in the dirt again and got by Miles for another error.

It would have been a great play if she'd made a better throw, Derek thought, digging into the batter's box and waggling his bat. But he also knew how hard it was to make a good play when everyone's eyes were on you— *and they all wanted you to fail.*

He shook his head, but then let go of it, because he had to concentrate on his own turn at bat. He had five swings to work with, and he wanted to make them count.

It wasn't too hard. Mason was throwing meatballs up there. Derek laced the first one to right, showing the coach he knew how to take the pitch the other way. The next pitch was in on his hands, but Derek got to it in time to hit another liner, this time right over third base.

"Nice!" Coach said, nodding his head and smiling. "Nice plate coverage, Derek!"

Derek tipped his cap in response and dug in again. This one was right over the middle, and Derek creamed it, way over the center fielder's head.

"Whoa!" Coach said, swiveling around to watch it go. "Power, too!"

Derek couldn't help smiling. Just to show the coaches everything he had, he bunted the next pitch perfectly down the third-base line. And for his final swing, he hit another one to right field, going with the outside pitch. He ran it out, going all the way to second and sliding in safely.

"Next!" Coach called, then turned and pointed to Derek. "Good hustle!" he said.

Derek clapped his hands twice and smiled again. Mission accomplished.

Practice was soon over, and Derek was glad about that. Every moment since he'd silenced Pete had been incredibly tense and awkward.

Derek now felt the other kids' eyes on *him* as well as Avery.

As they all gathered their things on the bench, Derek felt a tap on his left shoulder. Turning, he saw that it was Avery.

"I just wanted to say thanks." She looked quickly at him, then down at the ground.

He was about to say something encouraging, something positive, but then he saw Pete looking them and sneering. Behind Pete stood Harry, with a mocking look on his face.

"Ah, it was nothing," he told Avery, looking away to indicate that the conversation was over.

The less said between them right then, he figured, the better. He didn't want Pete and Harry and the others to get the wrong idea. He wondered if they already had. . . .

Derek could see that his response had stung her. She quickly turned away and headed for the curb, where the two older boys who'd come with her were waiting, along with a lady Derek took to be her mom. He watched as Avery went over to them, and the two older boys put their hands on her shoulders to comfort her.

Derek sighed. Now he felt *really* bad. He should have said something more to her—something to make her feel better.

He knew it. He just couldn't bring himself to ignore the stares he was already getting from the others. After all, he didn't want them to think . . .

It was a no-win situation, he realized. And things didn't look like they were going to get better anytime soon.

With Sharlee on cloud nine again after a great day of practice, Derek tried his best at dinner, but there was no hiding how upset he was. It was obvious, especially since Sharlee was in such a state of excitement. "Ciara and me are both pitchers!" she exulted.

"Ciara and *I*," Mr. Jeter corrected her.

"And we're both going to hit home runs every game— we decided!"

"Oh. Wow," Derek said, trying to share her excitement.

Of course, nothing got by his parents. Nothing *ever* did.

"Derek?" This from his mom, with a raised eyebrow thrown in.

"What's up with you tonight?" his dad asked with a penetrating look.

Pretty soon, Derek was forced to come out with the whole story. Well, not exactly the *whole* story. He told it casually, as if it were just another item mixed in with the pile of problems he had right now.

"A girl? Playing with the boys?" Sharlee's eyes sparkled—she could barely keep from levitating right out of her chair. "Can I go see her play? Daddy, can we *both* go?"

"I believe our game is at the same time that day," said Mr. Jeter. "So, it'll have to wait."

"Awww." Sharlee seemed disappointed, but of course she wasn't about to miss her game—not when she was scheduled to pitch *and* hit a home run.

"I have to say, I'm impressed," Mr. Jeter said. "Tell me, Derek—how have all the boys been reacting? How've they been treating her? With respect, I hope."

Derek swallowed hard. "Well . . . not really," he admitted. "I think she's having a pretty hard time, actually."

"She didn't exactly get a warm welcome?" Mrs. Jeter guessed.

"Yeah. You could say that."

"Well, I hope *you* weren't a part of that," his dad said, frowning.

"No!" Derek said, a little too quickly. "No, of course not, Dad. You know I wouldn't."

"Good," said Mr. Jeter. "It's very impressive, what she's doing. Very brave, if you ask me. I don't know if I'd have had the guts."

Derek's eyes widened. His dad had plenty of guts, Derek knew. He'd been in the military, and so had Derek's mom. For him to say that . . . !

"Well, I can see you're not happy about things," said Mrs. Jeter. "Is this part of it?"

"Kind of. I mean, it's really bad for the team. Everybody's distracted, and we've got a game on Saturday. . . ."

"You're exactly right, son," said Mr. Jeter. "You go out there and play focused, and you help your teammates do the same. That girl's as much a part of the team as any of them. Remember that."

"Yes, sir." He hadn't shared his *own* feelings about a girl being on the team. But somehow, his dad seemed to have guessed there might be some lurking doubts deep inside him.

Derek knew what his dad would have said to the team before their first game if *he* were their coach. He would have brought up the issue and laid down the law—and that would have been the end of it, once and for all.

But Derek's dad *wasn't* the coach.

• • •

Derek was so focused on his dad that he didn't realize his mom had left the room and gone into the kitchen—until he heard the dishes rattling in the sink. He got up and went in to help her.

She'd been awfully quiet tonight.

He started taking the dishes from his mom and drying them off with a towel before placing them on the rack.

"You know, old man," she said as she scrubbed a plate, "all people have the same feelings inside—girls, boys, whoever."

He nodded in agreement but didn't say anything.

"And if you want your team to be at its best, you should want—what's the girl's name?"

"Avery. Avery Mullins."

"Avery. Well, you should want Avery to play her best too. No team can be successful without every player pitching in, Derek. Everyone has to support everyone else so the team can play its best, just like in life: You need lots of support from the people around you if you're going to achieve your dreams—friends, family, teachers, teammates—everyone. And you should work to surround yourself with the people who are going to model that behavior and set that example for others. You need the right supporting cast."

Her words struck him. He wondered if she was talking about herself, not just Avery. He knew that her bosses had been avoiding her—he'd overheard her tell his dad one night. And they'd been dangling that promotion for a long time, even though she was clearly the most experienced person in the office, and the best one for the job.

His mom was the only woman in the accounting firm, Derek knew. He wondered if it was the same for her as it was for Avery. . . .

He wished he could go to his mom's office and tell everyone to treat her better. He wished he could tell them to promote her, because she deserved it!

Of course, he couldn't do that. On the other hand, he *could* do something about what happened on his *team*. . . .

Chapter Seven

REALITY HITS—HARD

Even though his mom was in the stands, and Vijay was right there with him on the bench, Derek felt somehow lonely as game one approached. He wished his dad could have been there to watch him play, even if he couldn't coach them. And Sharlee, too—Derek could always hear her voice, piercing through the crowd noise, cheering him on.

Vijay's mom and dad weren't there, but that was nothing new. They both worked in hospitals and put in crazy hours. Derek's family usually brought Vijay to and from Westwood Fields.

Derek saw that Avery had her mom with her this time—or at least, the woman Derek took to be her mom. There was no sign of the two older boys, though. Derek guessed they were probably involved in ball games of their own somewhere. He wondered if they were her brothers. They didn't look like her, but you never knew.

Right now, the Orioles were on the field having their warm-ups. They didn't look like as good a team as the Yankees, Derek thought as he watched them.

It was always nice to start off with a win, and this one looked totally gettable. With all the challenges the Yankees were facing as a team, they didn't need a tough game right off the bat.

After the Yankees took their warm-ups, Coach Stafford gathered them around for a pep talk. "Okay, guys—and girl." He cleared his throat before continuing. "Ahem. So, we'll start with Mason leading off and playing center, followed by Derek at short, hitting second. Then Pete, at second base, then Ryan at first, Tre' at third . . ."

Derek listened as the coach read out the names of his starters. He was glad to hear Vijay's name announced in left field—even though the coach had him batting dead last.

Avery's name was not one of those called. She was slated to begin the game on the bench. Derek saw her shoulders slump when Vijay's name was called, and she knew there were no more starting spots left.

Derek felt for her. She'd already gone through so much, and taken it like—well, like a *man.* He let out a chuckle.

Maybe they'll have to rewrite that saying, he thought. *Or even scrap it altogether.*

He wanted to tell her, "Hey, hang in there—you'll get in the game. Three other kids are on the bench, too—so it's not just you."

But he didn't say anything. There were other kids around, standing right there, and they would have heard him talking to her—which was more than any of them were doing. Only Vijay gave her a friendly clap on the back as he passed. She glanced up at him and smiled, then glanced at Derek.

He looked away, embarrassed—and then felt guilty about it. He would talk to her later and explain, or at least try to. Later, when there weren't a million people around who might take it the wrong way.

Derek hoped the coach would at least get her in the game. Avery had put up with a lot already—and she was definitely as good as Norman, who was starting in right field. Norman goofed off half the time in practice, clowning around with Elliott and Mark. The three of them didn't seem to care that much about the team winning. They were more interested in cracking one another up—often at Avery's expense.

Derek ran out to shortstop as the ump walked over to Harry and handed him the ball. "Play ball!" he shouted as he took his place behind JJ, the Yankees' catcher.

Harry was an intimidating pitcher. Derek had never hit

well off him, whether it was at the Hill or on opposing Little League teams. Harry had a buzzing, moving fastball and a wicked changeup to go with it. He'd been pitching since he was five, and he knew how to set up hitters. Derek was glad they were on the same team this season, so that he didn't have to face him.

The only thing was, sometimes Harry got too amped up. He tried to throw his fastball right through the catcher and into next week. And that made him wild.

As soon as Derek saw him walk the first batter on four straight pitches, not one of which was close, Derek knew this was one of those times.

It wasn't surprising, really. Harry wanted to show his coaches what he could do, and what a star he was.

But when Harry walked the second batter on six pitches—the poor kid swung and missed at two that were in the dirt—Coach K went out to the mound to calm him down. Derek and Pete walked over to hear what he had to say.

"Come on, kid!" Pete's dad told Harry. "What are you doing, huh? Get a grip on yourself. You've got great control—I saw you in practice. So, what gives? Let's go, huh? Get it over the plate!" He clapped Harry on the shoulder and headed back to the bench.

Derek jogged back to his position. He didn't think Coach K had done a very good job of helping Harry. If a kid was nervous, it wouldn't help to yell at him, would it? Derek couldn't imagine his dad saying stuff like that.

He saw Harry blow out a big breath, then try to throw the ball right over the heart of the plate. He succeeded—but the batter was waiting. He smacked it back up the middle for a hit that scored the first run for the Orioles. First and third, and still nobody out.

The next batter struck out, as Harry finally seemed to find his location. But the number five-spot hitter stroked a line drive toward Pete. Pete dove, and almost snagged it, but he landed hard and the ball trickled out of his glove.

When the runner at third saw it come free, he took off for home. Pete scrambled to his feet, grabbed the ball, and threw it—over the catcher's head! The second Orioles run scored, and the runner at first made it to second.

Harry was sweating, laboring hard to get through this rough start to the game. He got the second out on a fly to center, but Mason's throw to third was late as the runner tagged up.

With a man on third and two out, Derek thought they were out of the inning when the hitter popped up to shallow right. But as Pete and Ryan both went back after it, Derek could see they were headed for a collision. Both boys were looking skyward, yelling, "I got it! I got it!" But neither was giving way. Meanwhile, Norman, in right field, was keeping his distance, not wanting to be part of the impending pileup.

"Pete! Pete!" yelled Pete's dad, trying to call Ryan off.

But it didn't work. The two of them collided, and the ball fell to the ground between the boys.

Ryan quickly got up and fired it to second base, but the runner was already standing there. And of course, the man on third had long since scored to make it 3–0, Orioles.

Pete and Ryan started yelling at each other and at Norman, and Coach Stafford had to shout "Hey! Play ball!" before they quit it and went back to their positions, the argument still unsettled as to whose fault it had been.

Harry was steaming mad, Derek could tell—and he understood why. That last ball should have been caught, and Harry should have been out of the inning. But both Ryan and Pete had wanted to get the glory. Everyone, it seemed, was trying to be a star today.

Harry used his fury to focus on getting the third out. He struck out the hitter on three straight screamers right down the middle. Turbocharged by anger, his fastball had too much giddyap for the hitter to catch up with.

And so, finally, the Yankees came to bat. The Orioles pitcher was surprisingly good, Derek thought as he watched Mason strike out ahead of him.

Derek managed a line drive, but it went straight to the shortstop, who didn't have to move to make the grab. Pete struck out swinging for a one-two-three inning.

This, thought Derek, *is not how things were supposed to go down. Not at all.*

Harry kept the game close for the next three innings, holding the Orioles to just two singles over that span. But the Orioles pitcher was just as good. Only Vijay managed a hit—and it was a weak dribbler that happened to find the right spot. And then Mason struck out to end the third.

But in their half of the fourth, the Yankees finally mounted a rally. It started with Derek, who hit another line drive—this time straight back through the middle, making the pitcher dive for cover.

With Derek at first, Pete swung so hard he practically came out of his shoes. The result was a groundout to first. But at least it got Derek over to second. From there, he scored on a fly ball to center that was dropped for an error.

Ryan now stood on second base, with JJ up at the plate. A promising setup for another Yankee run, thought Derek as he stood cheering his team on. He noticed that Avery was up and cheering too.

JJ, Coach Stafford's son, was a good hitter. But speed was not his strong point. And so, when he smacked a ball into right, it took one bounce and came straight to the fielder, who threw to first, beating JJ there by a step!

The Yankees had to settle for one run. "I would have scored if you'd hustled and beaten the throw to first," Pete complained to JJ on their way to the bench. "You run like a snail."

"Why don't you just zip it?" JJ shot back.

Soon the sons of the two coaches were yelling at each other. Their fathers had to separate them and sit them down to cool off. Miles went in to play catcher, while Mark was sent out to second base.

But Avery remained on the bench, waiting her turn, along with JJ and Pete, who were seated on opposite ends. Elliott sat as far from Avery as he could, giggling. He seemed to think the fight between his teammates was a laugh riot.

Avery stared out at the field, no trace of a smile on her face. Derek knew how she felt. Their team was digging itself a hole, and they were in serious danger of losing to a weaker team.

Not to mention the fact that the coaches were making substitutions, but they weren't calling her name.

With the score 3–1, Orioles, and Harry having exhausted his pitch count, Coach Stafford brought Mason in to pitch, and sent Elliott out to center field. That left only one kid who hadn't yet gotten into the game—Avery.

Derek could see her leaning forward, fingers gripping the chain-link fence, staring out at the game. He saw Avery's mom in the stands with her hands cupped to her mouth, yelling something in the direction of the coaches. If Avery wasn't going to say anything, she certainly was, it seemed.

The top of the fifth inning was going to be crucial, Derek knew. If they could keep the score at 3–1, the Yanks had a chance with two turns left at bat.

But without their best pitcher, and with kids at second and in center who weren't strong fielders, the Yankees were vulnerable to a knockout punch.

And sure enough, that's what happened.

After four innings of whiffing at Harry's fastball, the Orioles had Mason timed perfectly from the start. Mason had good control as a pitcher, but he was smaller than Harry by a lot, and didn't throw nearly as fast. The first man to face him hit a short-hop grounder to second.

Mark, instead of trying to block it, jumped out of the way, as if it were a speeding truck.

The ball went into right field, where Norman threw it back in, but by that time, the runner was already on second.

Mason walked the next batter. Then, with men on first and second, he got a ground ball to short. Derek scooped it up and threw to second—but Mark dropped the throw, and everyone was safe!

Howls went up from the bench, where Pete had plenty to say, and from the field, where everyone, from Tre' to Ryan to JJ, was getting on Mark's case.

Avery, though, said nothing. She sat there on the bench, hands gripping the fence in front of her, staring out at the game, as if she were a prisoner waiting to be set free.

Mason got a pop-up for the first out, then a grounder to first that Ryan grabbed, stepping on the bag for the second out. But a run scored on each of those plays, making the score 5–1. And when Elliott dropped an easy fly ball to center, another run scored. By the time Mason struck out the next batter, it was 6–1, Orioles.

The Yankees went down in order in the bottom of the fifth, including strikeouts of Tre' and Elliott. Everyone had been trying way too hard to do way too much—instead of just doing their jobs and being mentally in the game.

With one inning left, and the game pretty much out of reach at 6–1, Coach Stafford finally put Avery in, substituting her for Mark at second, while moving Mark to left and sending Vijay to the bench.

Derek was sad that it had to be Vijay coming out of the game to make way for her. He'd been due to lead off next inning. But at least he'd played five innings and had a couple at bats. And this way, Avery would be sure to get an at bat, as well as play in the field.

Avery seemed relieved. From the stands, her mom could be heard shouting encouragement. Too bad Coach hadn't put her in last inning instead of Mark or Elliott, Derek thought. If he had, maybe they wouldn't be down five runs now.

Mason struck out the first hitter, then seemed to lose the plate and walked the next man.

The Orioles' cleanup hitter came to bat. Mason fooled him with a changeup for strike one. On the next pitch, the hitter got under it, sending a pop-up to short left field. Avery backpedaled, shouting, "I got it!"

But Tre', backpedaling from third, was also yelling "I got it!" and his voice was a lot louder. Hearing it, Avery backed off at the last minute, while Tre' dove for the ball—and missed it.

"Second base!" Derek yelled as he raced to cover the bag. They could still get the out if she threw to him in time.

Avery went for the ball, but just as she grabbed it, Tre' wrestled it out of her grip. By the time he fired to second, it was too late.

Moans went up from half the Yankees team, and even Coach K. "Thanks a lot," Derek heard Tre' tell Avery. "Talk about blowing it. That was my ball all the way."

Except it wasn't, thought Derek. Avery had been in much better position to make the play. She wouldn't have had to dive for it. Tre' had just assumed that if he left it up to her, she would blow it. And now that he'd blown it himself, he was blaming her—in front of everybody.

Avery didn't answer. Instead, she got right back into fielding position, pounding her mitt ferociously with her right fist, focused on whatever was going to happen next.

Mason, trying too hard, fired a wild pitch, and the runners advanced to second and third.

After getting a pop-up for the second out, Mason gave up an infield single to the next hitter for the Orioles' seventh run. Although he got the next batter to ground out, the damage was done. The Yankees now had a seven-run mountain to climb, not six—with only three outs left. Was it too late? Or did they still have a rally left in them?

Derek stared through the chain-link fence as Avery stepped into the box. She swung the bat around like she'd been watching the pros on TV. And when she took a rip at the first pitch, she looked good doing it—even though she swung right through it.

To Derek's dismay, some of the Yankees let out a mock cheer. He heard Norman saying, "And it's outta here!" which got a laugh from more than a few of his teammates.

If Avery heard any of it, she gave no sign. Her concentration, as usual, was intense. And with a 2–1 count, she made the doubters look bad, turning around a high fastball with a wicked swing that sent a screaming liner over the second baseman's head for a single.

Derek quickly grabbed his bat and headed to the on-deck circle. Mason worked a seven-pitch walk, and suddenly, the Yankees' bench was alive with excitement. Even kids like Elliott and Norman were into the game now.

Derek stepped to the plate and took a deep breath. He waggled his bat around and took a few practice swings to work off the excess tension. In came the first pitch—and Derek let it go. He hadn't seen this pitcher before, but the kid had already walked one batter. Derek was willing to take a walk here and leave it up to the kids behind him.

But he wanted to make sure that if he got his pitch, he was ready for it. Lo and behold, the next one was chest-high and over the heart of the plate. Derek lashed it past the second baseman, and Avery scored easily. Mason, at third, pointed at Derek, who stood on first clapping his hands.

Still nobody out, and the score was now 7–2. Mark stepped to the plate. Derek wished it had been Pete up there. Pete had a ton of power, and usually made good contact. Mark, on the other hand, had trouble getting around on the fastball—and he showed it by swinging through three straight pitches for the first out.

Now Ryan, another big hitter, stepped up to the plate. He belted the first pitch a mile, but it landed just foul in left field. Foul or not, Ryan's blast seemed to spook the pitcher. His next four pitches were all away, giving Ryan nothing to swing at. He walked to first, and the bases were loaded!

Derek was always careful in these situations not to get overconfident. But he couldn't help feeling excited as the Yankees' rally gained steam. It was as if a sleeping giant had awakened. Was it just in time—or was too late?

Miles lashed a single to left on a 2–1 count. That sent Mason scooting home, with Derek close behind. "Yeah!" he shouted, exchanging high fives with the rest of the team—including Avery.

The rally was in full bloom now, with the score 7–4 and runners on first and third with only one out. The Orioles' coach came out to the mound and signaled a pitching change. The downcast pitcher went to the bench, and in came a kid who was much bigger. Derek even thought he could make out the beginnings of a mustache on his face!

The coach handed him the ball, and he threw a few to the catcher to warm up.

Missiles.

Tre' was up next. The first two pitches had him ducking for cover. Everyone winced, but luckily, they missed him by inches. After two more balls, one away and one in the dirt, Tre' headed to first to load the bases again.

Next up was Elliott, who looked totally terrified—and no wonder. The pitcher was wild and throwing lasers. Sure enough, his first pitch hit Elliot in the bicep and sent him into a screaming, yowling fit of pain that might have been dramatized for effect, but was still real, Derek was sure.

Now it was 7–5, and still only one out!

Derek was beginning to feel like his team had a date with destiny today. Sure, the bottom of their order was up, and the pitcher was throwing fireballs. But if he didn't start throwing strikes soon, the Orioles were doomed.

Norman ducked and hid as the first pitch curved inside. On the second pitch, he twisted away to avoid a high fastball—but the tip of his bat hit the ball and sent it squibbing down the first-base line!

"RUN!" everyone yelled. Norman got the message and headed toward first. The Orioles catcher ran to get the ball, then saw that it might go foul, and that if he picked it up, he'd be too late anyway. So, he let it go . . . and the ball came to a stop right on the baseline!

Now they were only one run down. The bases were still loaded, and there was still only one out. All signs were pointing to a Yankees miracle.

Then up to the plate stepped Avery, for the second time that inning.

Derek whistled and clapped his hands, and the Yankees and their fans made lots of noise. *It doesn't matter* now *that she's a girl, does it?* he thought, watching his teammates cheer her on.

He knew she was going to hit the ball hard. He could tell by her focus, and the way she stood in the box, still and poised, waiting for the pitch. . . .

It was high and hard, and a tough pitch to hit—but Avery made solid contact. The ball jumped off her bat and just to the right of the Orioles' shortstop. He went airborne . . .

And came down with the ball!

Derek had been on the point of jumping for joy, but he froze, his joy turning to agony.

And there was even worse to come. The shortstop sprang back up quickly and fired to first. The ball got there just before Norman, who had been slow to realize the ball was caught and had to get back in a hurry.

"OUT!" yelled the ump. "Double play!"

And just like that, the game was over!

• • •

The Yankees had fallen short—on a great play, to be sure, but that didn't matter now.

She hit that ball right on the nose, Derek thought. Nine times out of ten, it would have won them the game. It *should* have—but it didn't.

To most of the Yankees, Avery was now the scapegoat. Not only did she not belong here, playing in a league full of boys, but as far as they were concerned, she'd also made the final out that cost them their first big game.

"Thanks a lot," Derek heard Harry say.

"Way to ruin everything." This from Pete.

"Next time take one for the team," Ryan muttered.

"Next time stay home," Norman piled on.

They were being *awful*, Derek thought. He couldn't just sit there and let it go on—he had to say something to her.

He walked over to where she sat on the bench, looking down at her lap and fiddling with her mitt. "Hey."

She kept her head down, ignoring him.

"Hey!" he said again.

"I have a name," he heard her say, though she still didn't look up.

Derek corrected his error. "Sorry. Hey, Avery."

She looked up at him, finally. "What?" She was already defending herself, and she didn't even know what he was going to say.

"Good game. You hit that ball really well off that guy, and he was throwing bullets."

"I lost us the game," she said, looking back down.

"That guy made a great play. Nothing you can do about a thing like that. It's just bad luck, that's all. Not your fault, anyway."

That got a grateful smile out of her. "Thanks. Thanks for that," she said. "Hey," she added, getting to her feet. "Mind if I ask you something?"

"Uh . . . sure," he answered, looking around to see whether the other kids were staring at the two of them talking.

Avery looked around too—and saw something that made her say, "Oh no."

Derek turned and saw what she was staring at. The woman who'd driven Avery to the game—her mom, he assumed—was talking to the coach, and it seemed like anything but a friendly conversation. She was flailing her arms around, and her voice was getting loud.

Before he knew it, Avery had dashed over there to head things off before they went any further.

Derek could understand where she was coming from. No kid wants their mom or dad fighting their battles for them. He watched as she pulled her mom away—and so did all the other boys.

Feeling like he was watching somebody else's private business, Derek looked around and saw his own mom.

"You guys almost caught them, old man," she said, putting an arm around his shoulders. "Come on. Let's go home. You'll get 'em next time."

Derek cast a look back as they left for the car. Avery was standing face-to-face with her mom, complaining to her. He felt like he could almost hear her, word for word. "Let me handle this myself!"

But holding her own on a team full of hostile boys—that was a battle that might not be winnable.

Chapter Eight
ALL WORK AND NO PLAY

Sharlee and Mr. Jeter arrived home just minutes after Derek.

"We won! We won!" Sharlee said excitedly. "And I hit a single and another single! And Daddy is the best coach—he told me to go to second, so I did, and then the single was a double! Right, Daddy?"

"Right, Sharlee," her dad said with a chuckle.

"How was your game, Derek?" his dad asked. Derek looked away. "Oh," said Mr. Jeter. "Not so good, I guess."

"We lost," Derek said. "And they were way worse than us!"

"What happened, then?"

"We messed up." Derek pounded one of the sofa pillows three times to let off some steam.

"How did you personally do?"

"I did fine, but so what?"

Mr. Jeter smiled. "I know. It's all about the team, isn't it? Well. Sorry I couldn't be there, son. I'll be at the next one, though. Sharlee's game is later that day."

"Me too?" Sharlee asked, putting her palms together in prayer. "Please?"

"Sure!" said Mr. Jeter. "You and I, we'll go together and root for Derek."

"And for Avery!" Sharlee said pointedly. "Did she play good?"

"Did she play *well*," Mr. Jeter corrected her.

"Well, did she?" Sharlee asked.

Derek shrugged. "She didn't play much—just one inning. But she did okay—no worse than anybody else."

"That's not fair!" Sharlee said, pouting and folding her arms across her chest. "Your coach is bad—he should let her play more. Then she'd get better!"

"You're probably right, Sharlee," Derek allowed. "She actually hit the ball pretty well—but it didn't work out, and the guys all blamed her for it."

"Oh," said Mr. Jeter, frowning. "I see. Hmmm . . ."

"If I'm coming to the game, I want to see her play," Sharlee said firmly. "I think she's cool. Who cares what those stupid boys think, anyway?"

"Now, Sharlee," said her dad, "don't be calling people stupid."

"If they're blaming her for losing, and it was their fault, not hers, then they *are* stupid."

"Sharlee," Mr. Jeter warned.

"Okay, okay. But I still want to see her play. And I'm going to make a big sign that says, 'GO, AVERY!'"

"*That's* a good idea," said her dad, patting her on the back. "Now you've got your thinking cap on."

"Daddy, next year, can I play baseball too?" Sharlee asked.

"Well, maybe not next year. But later on, if that's what you want, of course you can," Mr. Jeter said.

"Because Charlie Willis, in school? He told me girls *can't* play baseball, only softball. He's mean."

"Sharlee," Mr. Jeter said, chuckling in spite of his disapproval, "what Charlie doesn't understand is that there's nothing about softball that means it isn't as good as baseball. It's just that up until now, most girls have gone out for softball. It's hard being the first to do something—it can be lonely. If Avery wants to play baseball with the boys, and go through all that, she must have a really good reason."

"What kind of reason?" Derek asked. "I've been trying to figure that one out."

"Maybe you ought to ask her," his dad suggested. "You might be surprised by her answer, if she's willing to share it with you."

"I was *going* to ask her. . . ."

"But?"

Derek shrugged. He didn't want to tell his dad about Avery's mom arguing with the coach. He wasn't even sure she *was* her mom. Anyway, it was none of his business.

"I don't know," he said. "Something else was going on. I forget what."

Ask her yourself, his dad had said.

Well, maybe he would.

"Ugh," Derek muttered as he sat cross-legged on the floor of his bedroom. In front of him, strewn all over, were pieces of corrugated cardboard, tubes of glue, staplers, and toothpicks. "This is the biggest pain ever!"

Gary had given him sketches of what the mouse maze was to look like—complete with measurements in his scrawling handwriting that took Derek almost an hour to decipher.

Now, he was finding out that cutting corrugated cardboard with scissors is really, really hard. His hand was aching so badly, he had to shake it out every few minutes. If he'd had a proper tool, it might have been easier. But what did he know about tools for arts and crafts?

He'd asked his mom, and she'd told him about something called a matte knife. But did they have one in the house? Nope. And neither she nor his dad had time to drive him to the craft store or the hardware shop downtown.

His dad was grading essays, and his mom had taken paperwork home from her job. She was still trying to show her bosses how much harder she worked than everyone else, so they would give her that promotion. But every day that went by, she got more and more discouraged.

There were about thirty pieces of cardboard cut to fit the maze—but now Derek's hand was cramping up, and he could go no further. With a moan of frustration, he headed downstairs. "Dad!" he said. "I need a matte knife or whatever. Can you take me to the store?"

"I could take you a little later, Derek," he began. "But if you need one right now, why don't you try asking Mr. Wheeler over at 517? He's got all kinds of tools lying around." Mr. Wheeler was their neighbor three doors down in Mount Royal Townhouses. He was retired, kind of—but he still did odd jobs for the neighbors who needed a little help.

"Good idea," said Derek. He wished he could pay Mr. Wheeler to do the whole maze for him, so he could get his work done and go play ball out on the Hill. But he knew that wasn't about to happen. Still, it was worth asking to borrow a cutting tool.

Five minutes later, he was back, matte knife in hand. Now the work went faster, but still, by the time he finished the outer walls of the maze—his target for the afternoon—it was too late to head for the Hill. The sun was already setting. Soon they'd be sitting down to dinner.

"Aaargh!" he groaned. "Why? Why me? Couldn't Ms. Terrapin have assigned somebody else to be my partner? Did it *have* to be Gary?"

Derek knew Gary would wind up putting in less time than him on their project. That had been Gary's whole plan from the beginning, of course. Because that was how he operated. Gary was a legend in his own mind, the star of his own imaginary show. And on the Gary Parnell show, there was no supporting cast. Everyone else was just there to help him shine.

Chapter Nine
HEAVY BLOWS

Derek and Sharlee were helping set the table when his mom came home from work that Monday evening. Mr. Jeter, who was at the stove cooking up a pot of chili, looked up as she came into the kitchen and saw at once that something was wrong.

"You okay, Dot?" he asked, a look of concern on his face.

Mrs. Jeter sniffed. "I'm fine." She kept right on going, back into the hallway. "Just gotta wash up."

"Derek," said his dad, "keep an eye on that chili. Call me if it starts to boil over." Taking off his apron, he went to follow his wife.

"What's going on?" Sharlee asked Derek.

"Nothing. I don't know. Just forget about it."

It took a while for them to come back in, but luckily the chili stayed in its pot and didn't boil over. Mrs. Jeter sat down at the table, while Mr. Jeter went to the stove and got a ladle to serve the chili.

"Kids," she said, taking each of their hands in one of hers, "today was not a good day for me. So if I don't talk much, I hope you'll understand."

"Mommy, did somebody die?" Sharlee asked, looking worried.

"No, no, honey, nothing as bad as that. I just . . ." She sighed heavily.

"Your mom was passed over for her promotion," said Mr. Jeter.

"You mean she didn't get it?" Sharlee asked.

"That's right," Mrs. Jeter said. "They promoted somebody else instead. A very nice young man."

"Even though he's only been there one year, and isn't as qualified as your mom is," said Mr. Jeter.

"But I don't get it," Sharlee said, screwing up her face in an effort to understand.

"Some things are hard to understand, Sharlee," said Mrs. Jeter.

"And hard to explain," added Mr. Jeter.

Sharlee didn't seem at all satisfied, but Derek knew what they both meant. He thought of how it was similar to his team's situation with Avery.

He still wished there wasn't a girl on his team—although it was getting harder and harder to say *why*. But there was. And he had to deal with it. Just like she had to deal with prejudice and unfair treatment—like his mom.

Not for the first time, he wondered why things were the way they were, and wished they could be different.

"You deserved that promotion, Mom," he said, taking her hand again. "We all know it. And we all know why you didn't get it."

"I don't!" Sharlee complained. "Somebody *tell* me!"

"Sometimes people don't get treated right, and it's not fair," Derek told her. "That's what happened to Mom. It makes me so mad! I feel like going in there and telling them how blind they are."

"Aww." His mom hugged him, tearing up. "Thanks, old man. It's great to have support when you need it the most."

Sharlee joined the hug, and Mr. Jeter, too. They stayed that way until the chili started boiling over.

It was Tuesday after school. Time for the Yankees' second game of the season. This time, Derek's dad was in the stands along with Sharlee, who had, as promised, brought along a big white cardboard sign with the words "GO, AVERY!" on it.

She looked as excited as Derek had ever seen her. He sure hoped the team—and Avery—came through for her.

He'd been thinking about Avery, especially since his

mom had lost out on her promotion. He realized that up until now, he'd barely spoken two words to her. He'd finally broken through after their first game, but then Avery's mom had gotten overheated with the coach.

Derek noticed that she'd dropped Avery off today, along with those two older boys he figured were her brothers. But she herself hadn't stayed. Maybe Avery had asked her mom to stay away, he thought. Too much of a distraction, worrying about whether she was going to blow up at the coach again?

Or maybe Avery's mom was just busy today with something else, like his own mom, who'd had to stay late at work for a meeting.

"Hey, Derek," Vijay called to him. "Let's toss it around."

They started playing catch to warm up their arms, waiting for the rest of the ballplayers and fans to arrive.

"Hey, Avery!" Vijay motioned to her, inviting her to join them.

Vijay didn't care if the team had a girl on it, Derek noticed. He always just accepted everybody for who they were. Derek decided that if Vijay could be seen playing catch with her, so could he.

"You see that little girl over there with the sign?" Derek asked her, pointing over to Sharlee.

"Ha! Cute!" Avery said, cracking a rare smile.

"My sister."

"Really? Wow!" She seemed genuinely touched. "That's

so sweet." She turned and waved at Sharlee, who acted like she'd been singled out by the most famous ballplayer ever.

Avery waved again, then got back to business. Soon, most of the other kids arrived, and her rosy mood faded back to dark gray. Game time was approaching, and the Reds looked like a tough team to beat.

Derek decided that since he didn't really know her, he could only judge Avery by her play on the field, and the way she acted off it. So far, he had to say, she'd earned his respect.

If it were just him and Vijay, and others like them, who had to play with her as a teammate, it would have been okay. But it was her on the one hand, and Pete, Harry, Norman, Elliott, Ryan, and who knew who else on the other!

If only his dad had been their coach—the whole thing would have been straightened out by now. He was sure of it.

Coach Stafford and Coach K seemed not to want to deal with the problem. Were they just pretending not to see or hear what was happening? Didn't they care about the kids they were coaching? Didn't they care about the team?

Maybe it was because Avery's mom wasn't there, or maybe it was because she had argued with the coach. Either way, Avery began the game on the bench for the second straight time.

The Yankees were the home team again, so they started

out in the field. Derek was at short—apparently, he was going to play there all season, which was great with him.

JJ was behind the plate—the coach's son's chosen position, and why not? You had to be tough to be a catcher, and JJ was all of that. Big, too, with a strong arm. It came in handy in the first inning, when the Reds' leadoff man, having drawn a walk from Harry, tried to steal second.

Derek would have covered second and taken the throw, but knowing Pete, he'd glanced up to see if he, too, was covering.

He was, and it was a good thing Derek backed off, or one or both of them might have gotten hurt. Probably Derek, given Pete's size. As it was, Pete took the throw and tagged the runner out.

The better players on both teams all seemed to be playing well. The Yankees in particular seemed to be stepping it up from the sloppy play of their previous loss. This game was crisp, with well-hit balls being turned into outs by good fielding. It stayed scoreless into the fourth inning, although both teams had gotten plenty of runners on base.

In the fourth—Harry's last inning of work—he seemed to tire. His fastballs were up in the strike zone and very hittable. His breaking pitches were so far off the plate that hitters let them go for balls. He wound up walking two, and giving up a sharp single to right that scored the first run of the game.

With runners at first and third and still nobody out, Harry seemed to slump on the mound. When his first pitch nearly hit the batter, Coach Stafford had had enough. He came out to the mound and signaled for Mason to come in from center and take over. Harry moved to third, and Tre' replaced Mason in center.

The players on the field had shifted, but the kids on the bench stayed right where they were. In a 1–0 game, with the team still winless, the coaches clearly wanted this game badly.

The kids on the bench saw what was happening too. Elliott and Norman seemed to have completely lost interest in the game. They started clowning around with each other, keeping just quiet enough to avoid the coaches' notice. Next to them, Mark was absorbed in manicuring his nails with his mouth.

And then there was Avery, alone at the far end of the bench, leaning forward with both hands gripping the chain-link, like a tiger trying to rip its cage apart. She stared out at the action, her desire to play written all over her face.

"We want Avery! We want Avery!" Derek heard the chant and knew it was Sharlee. In the Middle Ages, thought Derek, thinking of his history class, she would have been a great town crier.

Others had now picked up the chant, including the two older boys who'd come with Avery.

Mason threw strikes, at least. He got the first hitter to

ground out—and it would have been a double play if Pete hadn't bobbled it before securing the ball.

The bad part was, another run scored. It would have come in even if Pete had made the double play. But now there was only one out, with a man at second.

The next hitter, a lefty, slapped a grounder just to the right of second base. Pete, who had been playing the hitter to pull, still got to the ball. But for the second time in as many plays, he botched the chance for a double play, throwing the ball wide so that Derek had to do a stretch to catch it while still keeping his foot on the bag for the out.

If Pete's throw had been true, it would have been an easy double play to end the inning. Instead, the Reds had players on first and third with two out, and two runs already in.

Coach Stafford and Coach K were huddled together, having what seemed to Derek like a disagreement. Finally, Coach Stafford called time-out, and made another substitution—calling Pete to the bench and sending Avery out to second!

"What?!" Pete yelled, throwing his hands up in astonishment. "You're sending *her* in? For *me*?" Pete turned to appeal to his dad, but Coach Stafford put a hand on his shoulder and guided him to the bench, speaking quietly in Pete's ear.

There was no scolding in the coach's manner. No anger about Pete showing him up for removing him from the game. In fact, it looked to Derek as if the coach was *apologizing* for taking Pete out of the game!

Derek shook his head, while Pete grabbed a bottle of water out of the team cooler and stormed off, disappearing behind the stands.

"A-ve-ry! A-ve-ry!" Sharlee had started up the chant, and now the two boys joined in with gusto. Avery gave her cheering section a little wave. Derek thought he even saw a smile cross her lips before quickly disappearing as she took her position at second.

"You got this!" Derek called over to her, smacking his hand into the pocket of his mitt. "No sweat. Let's go, Avery!"

Avery looked back at him and nodded firmly, smacking her own mitt.

"Go, Avery!" Vijay called from right field. She lifted her cap and waved it over her head to thank him.

Sure, she'd been out there the last game, but just for one play. Now, with the game only in the fourth inning, she was going to be tested for real—and sooner rather than later.

Sure enough, on the very next pitch, the hitter slapped a sharp grounder between her and Ryan. Avery sprinted back and grabbed it on the edge of the grass.

"First! First!" Everyone was yelling at her to throw it there, but Derek could see that Ryan had slipped going to cover the base. He knew she had only one play—throwing to him at second.

"Second!" he yelled—too late. Avery had already thrown to first. Ryan, who was just getting there, dropped the throw. The lead runner scored from third, and the trailing runner made it all the way to third base.

Moans went up from the bench and from the Yankees in the field—especially Ryan, whose gestures made it plain that it wasn't him who'd messed up.

"You had the play at second, doofus!" he told Avery. "What were you thinking?"

Avery turned away from him and was now facing Derek. He pointed to her and said, "Nice play coming up with that ball."

This time, she didn't nod back. She looked quickly away from him, and Derek could see that she was clenching her jaw, trying to hold back tears.

He understood how she felt. All those kids shouting "First!" and "Second!" must have confused her. Now she was upset with herself for messing up and costing the team a run. But she had to be upset with the rest of them, too.

"Hey, that was a tough play," he told her. "Don't worry. We'll pick you up. You'll see."

She didn't look at him, but he saw her nod her head as she pounded her glove ferociously and got back into fielding position.

It was 3–0 Reds now, still with men on the corners and two out. Mason buckled down and struck out the next hitter, thankfully.

And that gave the Yankees at least a decent chance.

The fourth inning started with Harry at bat. He'd struck out his first time up, but this time, he lofted a weak fly ball that dropped behind the third baseman for a leadoff single.

"Let's go! Let's go!" Coach Stafford shouted, clapping. "Come on, Yanks!"

The rest of the Yankees chimed in, getting the excitement revved up. Derek caught a brief glimpse of Pete, peeking out at the action from behind the stands. It looked to Derek like he'd been crying.

Next up was Tre'. He grounded out to the first baseman, but that got Harry to second. Miles struck out, and that brought up Vijay. Not the strongest hitter, but he usually made good contact—especially since being coached by Derek's dad the year before.

This time, he sent a dribbler down the third-base line. The catcher and the third baseman both went for it. The catcher got there faster and threw to first—wild. It got past the first baseman, and Harry scored easily, while Vijay went all the way to third!

Mason came to the plate, and the infield crept closer. Mason was a little guy, but Derek knew he had good strength for his size. Sure enough, he managed to hit it hard enough that it got by the infielders, scoring Vijay for the team's second run.

Now it was Derek's turn with two out and Mason on

first. He took three pitches, two of them strikes, to give Mason time to steal second and get himself into scoring position. On the third pitch, Mason went for it.

The Reds' catcher fired, right on the money. But Mason was too fast for him. "Safe!" the umpire yelled.

Now all Derek needed was a single to tie this game up. But he was down in the count, 1–2, and had to protect the plate, swinging at anything close.

The pitch came in. Derek saw quickly that it was a changeup, and adjusted his swing, waiting for it, then smacking it into right field. Mason scored, and Derek took second base on the throw. Tie game!

Standing on second, he clapped his hands and yelled, "Let's go, Avery!"

She stepped into the batter's box, waggling the bat and blowing out a long breath to calm herself.

Just a single, Derek thought. *Just get it past the infield, and I'll do the rest. . . .*

The pitch came in, and Avery hammered it, a long way!

Just her luck, it was close enough to the center fielder for him to make the play for the final out of the inning. What had started out as cheers when she hit the ball turned into more groans as she came slouching back to the bench to get her mitt.

Mason had a great fifth inning, getting three men in a row to pop out to the infield. But the Yanks went down just as easily in their half, with two men striking out and the third called out stealing after drawing a walk.

In the sixth, Mason had to face the heart of the Reds' order. And by now, he was getting tired. They lit him up for a pair of singles before he recorded his first out, a strikeout.

Things were as tense as they could be in Yankees Land. The Reds were threatening to retake the lead, and the Yankees didn't really have a number three pitcher. Derek had the funny feeling that it would be him, if it came to that. He sure hoped it didn't. He hadn't practiced pitching at all in the past year, concentrating on fielding and hitting.

Mason threw one in the dirt, and the runners advanced to second and third.

The next hitter grounded to Avery. "Home! Home!" Ryan and JJ both yelled. Avery, who had been about to throw to first for the sure out, turned and saw that the runner was already halfway home. She must have thought it was too late to get him, because she turned and threw to first, just in time to nip the runner for the out.

The Yankees groaned in frustration—but not Derek. He thought the runner would have scored anyway, especially since JJ would have had to tag him out because there was no force at home. He thought she'd made the right choice throwing to first—but apparently nobody else on the team agreed with him.

Now it was 4–3, Reds, and they were looking for more with a runner at third and two out.

Derek thought Coach Stafford was about to take Mason out of the game. He had one foot on the field and one on the sidelines, itching to call time-out. But for some reason, the coach never did yank his pitcher, leaving Mason in there for one more fateful batter.

Mason didn't have much left in his arm, that was for sure. The last two hitters hadn't seen a single fastball, and neither did this one. He was whaling away at Mason's lobs—luckily, fouling them off so far.

But with two balls and two strikes, the hitter creamed one over Derek's head—or was it? Derek leaped at the last minute . . . and came down with the ball sno-coning out of his glove! He quickly put his other hand on it to secure the catch.

"Out!" cried the ump. And the inning was mercifully over.

Derek accepted the high fives from his teammates. No one spoke to Avery, though, in spite of the nice play she'd made on that grounder for the second out. Derek's great play had made that one a distant memory.

Just one run to tie, and two to win! They had a more than decent chance, but his teammates seemed downcast, having lost the lead.

"We can do this!" Coach Stafford shouted, clapping his hands.

"Woo-hoo!" Derek chimed in, and Vijay joined him.

Derek looked around for Coach K, and spotted him on

the side of the stands, talking to Pete, who still seemed stricken by his removal from the game in favor of a girl. Derek thought he was being a baby, but he had to admit he wouldn't have liked it one bit if it had been taken out for *anybody*.

Tre' led off and lashed a clean single to left. Miles followed with a tapper to the mound. The pitcher had to go to first for the out, and Tre' advanced to second.

Vijay stepped up to bat. Derek yelled his lungs out urging his friend on, and the stands sounded off too, especially Derek's cheering section, led by Sharlee.

"Come on, Vijay!" Derek heard Avery yell.

Vijay swung hard at the first pitch—and missed. He rubbed his hands on his uniform pants, as if they were slippery from sweat, and gripped the bat tightly. On the next pitch, he swung even harder. The ball traveled about ten feet in front of the plate. Vijay ran, but he had no chance. The catcher checked to make sure Tre' wasn't going anywhere, then threw to first for the second out.

Only one out left. The team was desperate now. They had to score, or it would be over and done.

Mason sent a slow grounder toward third. The third baseman charged it and threw to first—but Mason was too fast, and beat it out for an infield single, with Tre' cruising into third easily.

Derek came up to bat, thinking, *Just a single, just a single . . .*

He heard the cheering somewhere off in the ozone, as he stepped into the box and focused on the pitcher.

Here it came . . .

Derek swung—way too hard. The ball skittered off the very end of the bat, rolling to the right of the pitcher.

Derek took off for first for all he was worth. He could see that Tre' was heading home, too.

The pitcher had to choose which way to throw. He had a play at the plate, with a slow runner—or he had a play at first where no tag would be needed.

The trouble was, he never got a handle on the baseball. As he reached down for it, he looked up at Tre' coming home—and missed the ball! The tying run scored, and Mason slid into third.

Now it was up to Avery. She stood in the box and let two strikes go right by her, while some of the Yankees on the bench moaned and groaned and complained, and the coaches ignored them, as usual.

Then she swung, popping one up to the infield. Three Reds players converged on it, while Avery hung her head and ran toward first dejectedly.

"I got it! I got it!" the three Reds all shouted. And they all did—that was the problem. The third baseman got his glove on it first, but he was elbowed aside at that instant by the catcher. The ball popped out of his mitt and into the air. The pitcher, who had also tried for the pop-up, dove for the ball but missed, and it hit the ground.

By that time, Mason had crossed the plate, and was jumping into the arms of his delirious teammates! Game over—Yankees 5, Reds 4!

Avery stood at first, watching the celebration around home plate. But she didn't join in. She just walked straight back to the bench and sat down to change out of her cleats.

Derek couldn't tell if she was crying or not. Her fans in the stands were all the way across the infield. Derek was much closer—so he left the happy pileup and went over to sit down next to her.

"You okay?" he asked.

"Why, do I look okay?" she shot back, still tying her shoe.

"You played really well today."

"I stunk up the joint."

"No you didn't," Derek said. "You did fine. Some tough plays there, is all."

She made a face and shook her head, as if he was talking nonsense.

"Hey, can I ask you something?"

"Sure. What?"

"How come you put yourself through all this? You could be playing softball instead. There's nothing wrong with playing softball, is there?"

Avery didn't answer at first. Then she said, "It's not the same thing. Not to me."

"Why not, though?"

"I've got my reasons." She furiously wiped a tear from her eye, as if it were a fly she wanted to swat.

"Okay . . . well, I'll see you next game, then."

"Yeah. Thanks." She finally looked up at him. "No, really, Derek. Thanks. I mean it. You're all right, you know?"

He didn't know what to say, so he just nodded and got up to go. What was it about Avery, that she wanted to play baseball so bad, she was willing to be tormented for it?

Chapter Ten
SHOWDOWN ON THE HILL

"Come on, Derek—we're already late!" Vijay stood in the doorway of Derek's living room, wearing his mitt and baseball cap, a bat tucked under his arm. "Harry's probably already there."

"I know, I know—it's just . . ."

Derek spread his arms out to show Vijay the cause of the delay. In front of him, on the living room coffee table, sat the mouse maze. Scattered everywhere were small pieces of cardboard. Derek's hands were covered in glue. A crumpled piece of paper towel hung from his right hand—and when he tried to remove it, it stuck to his left hand instead.

"Oh gosh," Vijay said, furrowing his brow. "Are you even going to come play today?"

"I just finished, believe it or not," Derek said. "It's a good thing, too. The construction part of my brain is fried."

"Why isn't Gary doing any of the work?"

"Because—he says it was his idea, and he's going to buy the mice and run the experiment at his house."

"Oh. Still, that seems kind of easy, compared to—"

"Don't get me started," said Derek, getting up off his knees and going to the kitchen to wash his hands off. "I'll just be a minute or two."

"Okay, but hurry it up. We've only got a couple hours before dark!"

"Ugh. And I'm going to have to start writing up the report on it. That's part of my job too."

Why did I agree to such a lopsided arrangement with Gary? What was I thinking?

Something was different. Something was *wrong*.

There were already a bunch of kids playing ball on the Hill—he could see that even from a long distance. A lot more kids than usual.

On a normal afternoon during the week, they'd usually have five or six kids, maximum. But there were at least a dozen out there. And as he and Vijay got closer, Derek noticed that very few of them looked familiar. . . .

"Hey!" he said. "Who are all these kids?"

"I have no idea. They look *older*, kind of."

Vijay was right. They *did* look older, by at least a few years.

Most of them, that is. One kid, out in the outfield, seemed smaller than the rest—more like Derek and Vijay's size. Other than him, though, these were all older kids. And they were on Jeter's Hill! "Hey!" Derek said to the kid who was catching. "Hey! This is our field!"

"Oh yeah?" said the kid, who was a whole lot bigger than Derek or Vijay. He took off his catcher's mask and looked at them with a challenge in his eyes. "Since when?"

"Since always!" Derek shot back. "Right, Vijay?"

"Yes!" Vijay agreed. "In fact, it is called Derek Jeter's Hill—and this is Derek Jeter right here!" He pointed to Derek, as if that proved their case.

"What, do you have a special permit or something?" the kid asked. The pitcher and the batter stood behind him now, all of them looking at Derek and Vijay.

"Um, no!" Derek said. "Who said we need one?"

"Exactly!" said the catcher. "Who said *we* need one either?"

"But we were here first!" Derek said, his voice rising along with his temper.

"Not today," said the catcher. "Today, you were here second."

"Well, what are you doing here, anyway?" Derek asked, knowing he had no good answer. "Do you guys even *live* around here? You don't look familiar."

"We're from over on the south side. Our field is getting renovated—they just started digging it up this week. So . . ."

"So you decided to come over here instead," Derek finished for him.

The kid shrugged. "What are you gonna do?"

"Well, we challenge you for it!" Derek said.

"You and whose army?" said the pitcher, joining in the debate. "I only see two of you."

"Well, there's two more coming now!" Vijay said, pointing to where Harry and Jeff Jacobson were walking down the path toward them.

"And here come three more," Derek said, pointing in the other direction, where another group of Hill regulars were already holding their arms out as if to ask, "What's going on?"

"Okay, you can challenge us," said the catcher, who seemed to be the leader of the group occupying the Hill. "After we finish our game."

"What?" Derek said. "It's already four thirty!"

"It's the last inning," said the catcher. "Cool your jets." He put his mask back on and got back into position behind the plate. The pitcher wound up and threw.

The hitter whacked the ball into center field, where the kid who was Derek's size made an incredible run at it and snared it with a full-out diving catch, somersaulting to his feet and throwing it in triumphantly.

The other players cheered. "Way to go! Woo-hoo!" they all shouted—even those on the opposing team.

"Wow," said Harry, after Derek and Vijay had explained

to the others what was going on. "Looks like we're going to have to get here early from now on."

"At least until the renovation on their field is over," Derek said.

"What a total drag," said Jeff.

"I hear you," Derek agreed.

The inning—and the game—ended with another great play by the little kid in center, who went back on a ball and made an over-the-shoulder catch, snaring it in the webbing of his glove like a sno-cone, then holding it up for everyone to see.

As the center fielder ran in and high-fived all his teammates—and the opposing players, too!—Derek suddenly realized the kid looked familiar. And when the kid took of his cap, and all that long hair tumbled out, Derek's jaw hung open in amazement.

It was Avery!

He hadn't even *recognized* her out there! The girl who was so tentative in the field in Little League seemed so relaxed and self-confident here, among boys who were two or three years older. Derek had never seen her smile like she was smiling now.

"Holy mackerel!" Harry said, blinking in astonishment.

"Unbelievable!" Jeff said.

"She's really, really good!" Vijay said with a broad grin.

The catcher came over to Derek. "Okay," he said. "You've

got six guys, we've got ten. I'll give you two of ours, so it's eight on a side. What's your name, anyway?"

"Derek."

"Jose," the catcher said, giving Derek a nod. "Nice meeting you." He then chose two boys, one of whom Derek recognized as part of Avery's cheering section.

"Hi," said the kid, offering Derek his hand. "Max Jonas."

"Derek Jeter," said Derek, accepting the handshake.

He saw Avery looking at him, and glanced away, a little embarrassed that he hadn't recognized her right away.

He spotted her other friend, who was part of the opposing team. He wondered how a girl his own age could have wound up playing with boys who were two or three years older.

The game began—with Avery pitching for the other side. In another surprise to Derek and the rest of his gang, she turned out to be a pretty good pitcher. She had a funky delivery, for sure. But it made it hard to pick up the ball out of her hand. Her pitches all had movement, too, making them hard to square up with the bat. Derek wound up grounding out, then striking out his second at-bat—which embarrassed him even further.

The game had a lot of good, tense moments, and great plays on both sides. But in the end Avery's team won by a score of 11–5. The eleventh run was provided by Avery herself, who hit a double to the opposite field to score the runner all the way from first base.

After the game, Jose came up to Derek, who was standing around stunned, like all the other Hill regulars. "Hey, don't feel bad," Jose told them. "At least you guys don't stink. Pretty good for a bunch of kids your age, actually."

"Kids?" Derek repeated. As if these guys weren't kids themselves, even if they were older!

"Don't worry," Jose went on. "Next time, we can choose up teams from the get-go, and include everybody, okay?"

He clapped Derek on the back and walked away, joining the rest of his friends as they headed back to the south end of town, half a mile away.

"This totally stinks," Harry said dejectedly, watching them go. "I'm out of here. See you guys next time."

"At least they're going to let us play with them," Vijay said, stressing the bright side as usual.

"Oh whoopee," Harry said sarcastically. "Mighty nice of them, to let us play on our own field." He left, and so did the others.

"See you in class tomorrow, Derek," said Vijay. "My parents will be back from work, and I've got to do my chores before dinner—feed the pets, take out the garbage, et cetera."

Derek looked around. He'd thought he was the last one there—but he saw that Avery was still sitting at the base of the tree behind home plate that served as a kind of backstop. She was tying one of her sneakers, and now she looked up and saw Derek standing there.

"Oh. Hi." She gave him a tentative smile, as if she wasn't sure he wanted to talk to her.

"Hey." Derek paused. "You played amazing today."

"Thanks," she said, her smile more relaxed now. "It's a lot different from . . . you know."

"It must be tough."

She let out a sharp laugh—the kind that says it isn't the least bit funny. "You think?"

"Why do you do it, then? I asked you the other day, but you never answered. I mean, I just . . . I don't get it."

Avery looked him up and down. "You really want to know?" she asked.

Chapter Eleven

WHAT LIES BENEATH

"It's not that there's anything wrong with softball," she said. "I just . . . never played it when I was little. Never ever."

"Why not? I mean, you like baseball so much now, you probably would have liked it fine."

She shrugged. "My big brother was already playing baseball, and he needed a partner to play catch with in the driveway, so . . ."

"Oh. Okay . . ."

"Then he started to play real ball, and he and the guys let me play with them over on the south side."

They let her play because she was good, thought Derek, knowing that no self-respecting kid would let their ball game be ruined by including a little kid unless that kid could hold up their end.

"I guess I got used to it—and once I did, I just kept on playing," she said. "Until . . ."

She fell suddenly silent, and Derek sensed a dark shadow falling over her mood.

"Until what?" he asked.

She took a deep breath, then let it out. "He died."

"*What? How?* What happened?"

She swallowed hard. "Car accident. He had an older friend who was driving and texting . . ." She trailed off.

Derek looked down at the ground, not knowing what to do, or how to console her. He waited, letting her calm herself down at her own pace, until finally she was able to continue her story.

"He was going to be a star. My parents had it all planned out: how he would get a full scholarship to University of Michigan . . . then get drafted by the pros . . . the whole deal. . . . My mom totally fell apart."

"Of course," Derek said softly. "*Anyone* would have."

"She and my dad got separated after that. He lives in Chicago now."

"Wow . . ."

"So now it's just me and my mom. She's actually the original athlete in our family. But it was my brother who always coached me, and made his friends include me, and told me I could do anything if I wanted it enough . . .

and not to let anyone—*anyone*—tell me I can't."

Derek was blown away. No wonder she'd been willing to put up with so much, and fight through it to play the game! He'd admired her determination from the beginning—but now he saw how deep and powerful her motivation was.

She was the only other person on his team—or in the whole Little League—who wanted to win as much as he did!

"So . . . those two guys who come to the games with you—they're your other brothers?"

"My brother's best friends—Max and Roger. They kind of adopted me after . . . They're the ones who got me into baseball and convinced me to pick up where Jacob left off."

Derek shook his head slowly. It was a sad story, but it made him understand better why she put herself through all the snubs and insults. He bet if the other kids on the team knew what she'd just told him, they'd treat her differently.

She *could* have told them, he guessed. But he could see why she wouldn't want to—it would be like begging for sympathy, and Avery clearly wanted to earn their respect on her own.

"So, to answer your question . . ."

"Huh?"

"About why I went out for baseball instead of softball? It was because of Max and Roger—and Jacob. I never played softball, ever. I was always an athlete, but I was into soccer and lacrosse, some field hockey."

Derek thought about the difference between the Avery he'd seen play today, and the one who seemed so rattled on the Little League field. It was obvious why—here, she had the support and encouragement of her teammates. It made her play loose and relaxed, and the results were amazing.

And she could pitch, too! The Yankees could have used her on the mound in that first game they'd blown.

Derek suddenly noticed that the sun was about to set. It would be getting dark soon, and his parents would be expecting him home. He also realized that Avery would be walking home alone.

"Where do you live?" he asked her.

"Just over there, about nine blocks." She pointed west. "On Emajean Street near Michigan Avenue."

He knew that if he walked her home, he'd be late for dinner. But he wanted to make sure she got there okay. He could still get back before dark, he figured—if they both walked fast.

On the way, she told him more about her brother, and how she was playing ball for him—to live his dream.

Derek could totally relate—he'd always had a dream that some people thought was "unrealistic"—to become starting shortstop for the New York Yankees. So he certainly wasn't going to tell her *her* dream wasn't possible.

"Well, here we are," she said, as they reached another apartment complex that looked like it needed tending. "This is me."

"Well . . . I guess I'll see you at the game."

"Yup. Thanks for walking me home," she said, giving him a smile.

"Ah, well, it—"

"I know. 'It was nothing,'" she finished for him. "You always say that. But it *isn't* nothing. So, thanks again."

With a wave goodbye, she turned and walked to the front door.

Derek waved back. Then he jogged all the way back home.

"Where've you been?" his mom asked when he came in. "You're fifteen minutes late—it's almost dark."

"It's a long story," Derek said.

"We're listening," said his dad.

Derek saw that Sharlee was listening too. "Can we talk about this a little later?" Derek asked, with a subtle nod in his sister's direction. He didn't want to talk about it with her around. It was a pretty heavy subject, and she might be upset hearing about Avery's brother.

His parents got the hint. "All right," said his dad. "You can explain before bed. But it had better be good."

". . . So, at first, I wasn't really thrilled about having some girl on the team," Derek said as he sat on the couch, with his dad sitting facing him one of the matching armchairs.

Mrs. Jeter had gone upstairs to tuck Sharlee into bed, after ten minutes of complaining that she wanted to hear Derek's story, *especially* if it was such a big secret.

"But Avery is not just 'some girl,'" Derek explained. "She's motivated, she's dedicated, she has a passion for the game, and she's also *good* at it—when she isn't being psyched out by the guys on the team. They're really giving her a hard time."

"Have you spoken to the coaches about it?" his dad asked.

"They're being unfair to her too! They don't do anything about it. Plus, they keep her on the bench. By the time they put her in the game, she's so psyched out that she makes mistakes. Like even when she makes a good grab, she'll throw to the wrong base or something."

"Sounds like she needs to play more to get more comfortable out there," said Mr. Jeter.

"Totally!" Derek agreed. "She's better than half the guys on the team, Dad—I saw her play over on the Hill, and she was like a different player!" He sighed. "But if the coaches won't play her, what can *I* do about it?"

"Well, first of all, let me say that I'm really proud of you for wanting to stand up for her. That's really admirable. Based on what you're saying, it sounds like you ought to speak to your coaches. But it has to be at the right time, and in the right way."

"Avery's mom tried that," Derek said, "and it didn't work out too well. The coaches wound up shouting at her, and after that, they sat Avery down just as much as before. I think they didn't like it when she yelled at them."

"Well, there you are," said Mr. Jeter. "You just said it yourself. Nobody likes being yelled at—or even talked at—especially in front of people. If you're going to talk to them, it has to be in the right way, and at the right time."

"For example?"

"Well for one thing, it would be better to do it in private. And not during the game, when his mind is on other things, and there are lots of other people there. Maybe at a practice, for instance. Do you have one this week?"

"Tomorrow afternoon," Derek said, still finding the prospect scary.

"Remember, Derek—coaches, like all adults, have to be treated with respect. Check your contract on that one."

Derek didn't need to check the contract he'd signed with his parents. In exchange for obeying certain agreed-upon rules, they'd promised to back him and his big dreams to the hilt. He'd been sticking to those rules for years now, and he knew them by heart—including the one about respecting adults. And in return, his parents had done their part.

But this was a sticky issue, and Derek wasn't sure their help would be enough. Somehow, he was going to have to find the courage inside him to stick up for a girl *and* stand up to his coach.

"Now remember," his dad said, "in the end, it's the coach's decision who to put out there on the field. Not yours. You may not like his decision, but you can't control it, and you have to respect it."

Derek nodded. "Yes, sir."

"You shouldn't call out the coaches directly."

"Then what do I say?"

His dad thought for a moment. "Maybe you could say something about how you've noticed the other kids ragging on her and making it really difficult for her. Put the focus on the other kids, not what the coaches are doing. And if you don't get the answer you want, just accept it gracefully, and understand it's their decision, and you've done all you can."

"Yes, Dad."

"I'm glad you're concerned enough to do something about it, Derek. And let me ask you this—how has Vijay been treating Avery? I can't believe he would join in and make life hard for her."

"No, he's been fine with her," Derek said. "Vijay would never do things like that."

"Well, there, you see?" said his father. "You're not alone. You've got another ally on the team. So don't be afraid to speak up."

Derek shook his head again. "I *am* afraid, kind of," he

said. "I don't want to get yelled at like Avery's mom."

"You won't if you do it the right way," his dad assured him. "And you'll be acting like a role model for your sister, too. The way you treat girls will have a big impact on her."

Derek thought about that for a moment. He wished he could have stood up for his mom at her workplace— but there was no way he could have. On the other hand, maybe he could help Avery in a tough situation.

"Okay, Dad. I'll give it a try," he said.

"That's my boy," said his dad, giving him a smile. "That's what courage is—doing something even though you're afraid to."

"Dad?"

"Yes?"

"Do you think I should tell the coaches about Avery's brother? It might help them understand her better."

"No, Derek. Whatever you do, don't say anything about that. She confided in you, and that would be breaking a confidence. In any case, it's her story to tell if she wants to. It seems to me she wants to succeed on her own—not because people feel sorry for her."

Chapter Twelve
IN REVERSE

Derek thought back to his talk with his dad. He knew he needed to say something to Coach Stafford—Derek didn't think there was much chance of Coach K giving him a listen, since they'd rarely seen eye to eye in the past.

He wondered if this would be the right time. Practice wouldn't be starting for another ten minutes. Half the kids weren't even here yet. Coach seemed like he was in a relaxed mood, chatting with people he knew in the stands.

If Derek didn't get up the courage to say something now, when would he? Soon it would be too late, and he might never get another chance. It was now or never.

"Um, Coach?"

"What is it?"

"Could I speak to you for a minute . . . privately?"

"Sure, Derek. I've got a few minutes." He led him a short distance away, down the third-base line. "Okay. I'm listening. What's on your mind?"

"It's something I found out, that I thought you should know."

"Yes?"

"It's about Avery." Derek sounded to himself like one of Vijay's mice.

"Yeah? What about her? She sick or something?"

"Actually, that's what I wanted to tell you about," said Derek. "I saw her play—somewhere else—and Coach? She's like a different player!"

"Is that right?"

"She was playing with kids two years older than her, and she was as good as them, or even better! Plus, she can pitch—she's got a mean junk ball."

"Derek?"

"Yes, Coach?"

"I've got an idea. Why don't you just do your job, and let me do mine, okay?"

Derek was stunned. He really had thought the coach would want to know about Avery's skills. He was sure he hadn't been disrespectful, and that he hadn't chosen a bad time to talk to him. And yet, he'd utterly failed!

Derek turned to go, feeling himself getting red in the face. And that's when he noticed that Pete and Harry were standing just six feet behind him. They were whispering to each other and glancing at Derek with wide eyes.

Behind them, Norman and Mark were at it too—while Avery was staring at him with a look of worry on her face, as if she guessed what he'd said to the coach and was horrified that he'd spoken up.

Derek wished that he'd kept his mouth shut. But it was too late. There was no taking back what he'd said.

He ran to the bench, grabbed his mitt, and trotted out to shortstop for infield practice. His embarrassment still stung as he whipped the ball around to his teammates.

Harry and Pete were still laughing, and Derek was sure it wouldn't be long before the jokes started making the rounds about him and Avery.

Why, oh why didn't I make sure me and the coach were alone the whole time?

"Hello, it's me—your worst nightmare." Gary's smile made Derek think at first that Gary had finally gotten wise to himself and was telling a joke. But no such luck.

There he was, standing in Derek's doorway, holding a cage with a cover draped over it. "Very funny," Derek said, not laughing. "Come on in. The maze is all done. I nearly drove myself crazy finishing it in time."

"Well, good for you," Gary said. "Aren't you the diligent one." It wasn't a question, just a statement of fact. But Gary somehow managed to make it sound sarcastic.

Derek stepped aside so Gary could maneuver the cage past him and into the Jeters' living room.

The maze was set up on the coffee table. "Where should I put this down?" Gary asked.

"Over there, on the floor," Derek directed, pointing to a spot in front of the TV set.

"Nice job, Jeter," Gary said, setting down the cage and admiring the cardboard maze Derek had so painstakingly glued together in the exact pattern Gary had drawn up.

"Why'd you bring the mice?" Derek asked. "I thought we were going to wait until my mom or dad could drive me over to your house with the maze."

"Uh, yeah . . ."

"We're supposed to run the experiments at your house, right? That's what we agreed on, Gary."

"Wellll . . ." Gary winced comically. "Slight change of plans." He turned his palms upward helplessly. "Nothing I could do about it. My mom saw the mice I brought home, screamed her head off, and made me take them right back to the pet store!"

"What? But you said—"

"You want to try changing my mom's mind?" Gary offered. "It's never happened before, but I guess there's always a first time. If not, though . . ."

"If not, it's *my* mom and dad I'll have to convince," Derek said. "And that's not happening." Staring at the covered cage, he added, "You're saying it's empty?"

"Yup. That's what I'm saying."

Derek blew out a relieved breath. But then, reality sank right back in. "Gary, there is no way my parents are going to agree to have mice in here."

"Then we are sunk. Unless you want to go back to the drawing board and start over with one of my other project ideas?"

"No way! You guaranteed you would handle the mouse part of things! If we get an F, it's your fault!"

Gary cocked his head to one side. "Maybe. But you still get an F, Jeter. How are your parents going to like that?"

"You've got to do something! You're the one who didn't come through!"

"I know, I know," Gary admitted. "Look—if you get the mice, I'll write up the whole experiment, okay?"

Derek was beginning to panic, but just then the phone rang, breaking the tension at least for the moment.

"Hello?"

"Hi, it's me," Vijay's voice greeted him. "You going over to the Hill today? Those older kids are already there. Avery, too."

"I can't, Vij. I'm stuck here with Gary, doing our science experiment."

"Too bad," said Vijay. "Sheila and I finished ours last week. So, I am going to the Hill, as soon as I finish feeding my mice."

Ding! How had he not thought of it right away? Derek

asked himself. The solution had been staring him right in the face, in the person of his best friend!

"Hey, Vij?"

"Yes?"

Derek was about to ask him if he and Gary could use Vijay's mice for their project—but then he thought better of it. "Well, say hi to everybody over on the Hill," he told his friend. "I'll see you at the game tomorrow."

He hung up, then turned to face Gary. "Vijay has pet mice."

"He does? Great! We're saved!" Gary suddenly froze in mid-ecstasy. "Wait. Why didn't you ask him if we could use them? You were just talking to him!"

"I didn't ask him," said Derek, looking Gary straight in the eye, "because *that* is *your* job. In fact, so is the whole rest of this project—running the experiments, writing up the paper—the whole works."

"*What?* Why should I—"

"Because you welched on your part of the project, that's why. I found you some mice, right? Now keep your part of the bargain!"

"No fair!"

"Gary, I'm shocked!" Derek said, adopting Gary's haughty attitude. "Who told you that life was fair?"

Gary was speechless, his jaw hanging down.

"Vijay said he's already finished with his own project. Maybe if you offered to count him in as part of ours, too, he could get extra credit—that might convince him."

Gary furrowed his brow, thinking about it.

"Of course, you'll have to get Ms. Terrapin's okay, too—but she's usually pretty cool about stuff like that. I'm sure you'll have no problem convincing either of them."

"You'll pay for this, Jeter," said Gary, grabbing the cage and heading for the front door. "You'll be sorry you didn't cut me a break here."

"Okay, okay," said Derek, having had his fill of busting Gary's chops. "*I'll* ask Vijay. But you still have to ask Ms. Terrapin. And make sure she knows that Vijay deserves extra credit."

"Sure, I'll do it," Vijay told Derek as they sat in the back seat of the Jeter family station wagon. "Why not? Especially since I'm getting extra credit."

"Well, that's if Gary does his job for once, and gets Ms. Terrapin to agree."

"It will be good to get extra credit without having to do any extra work," Vijay said, smiling. "Especially since Sheila made me do all the work on our project."

"Just like Gary tried to do with me!" Derek said. "What is it with people, anyway? I thought Sheila always likes to take over everything."

"She likes to give orders, that's for sure," said Vijay. "She seemed to think I was there to work for her."

Derek's mom sat in the front seat, not saying much.

She'd been kind of down ever since getting passed up for her promotion, he'd noticed. Well, why shouldn't she be bummed out? *He* would have been, for sure.

"Hey, Mom," he told her. "We're going to win this game for you, okay? And I'm going to hit a homer in your honor, too."

"Aw, that's so sweet, old man," she said, smiling at him in the rearview mirror.

They got to the ballfield and piled out of the car. Mrs. Jeter went off to find a parking spot, while Derek and Vijay threw their mitts in the air and caught them as they ran toward home plate.

"Who are we playing today?" asked Vijay.

"Looks like the Red Sox."

"Yankees-Red Sox! The greatest rivalry in baseball!"

Derek laughed, but he knew today's game was no laughing matter. The Yankees were 1–1, and they were lucky to have won the game they did.

Derek's mom sat herself in the top row of the stands. She plopped down a cooler and a jacket on the bench next to her, to reserve those seats for Mr. Jeter and Sharlee, who would be coming as soon as their game was over.

A few seats down sat Avery's cheering section. They'd obviously gotten here early. Avery's mom was back after a one-game absence, along with Max and Roger.

If Avery's fan club had come to watch her play, they were soon sorely disappointed. When Coach Stafford read off his starting lineup, Avery wasn't on it, for the third straight game. Derek watched her shoulders sag in disappointment as she dropped down onto the bench.

Thankfully, the game soon got underway, and Derek was able to put his agonizing thoughts aside and concentrate on the task at hand.

The Yankees were up first, and right off the bat, they came out hitting. Mason smacked a clean single to right, and Derek followed with a ringing double that split the outfielders and scored Mason for the game's first run.

If Harry, Pete, and the others had been laughing at Derek before, they were all on board with him now. "Way to go, Jeter!" Harry called from the on-deck circle, while Pete, at bat, pointed his way in approval.

Pete hit a long fly ball that was run down by the left fielder, and Derek tagged up and made it to third. He scored on Harry's double down the first-base line, and Harry scored with two outs when Tre' singled to center.

Vijay struck out, but after half an inning, the Yankees had a nice, comfortable three-run lead.

"Go, Yankees!" Derek heard his sister's voice coming from the stands. Looking up, he saw her next to his mother, with Mr. Jeter seated on her other side. "Go, Avery!" Sharlee held up the cardboard sign she'd made herself. "GO, AVERY!! GIRLS RULE!!" it said.

Derek felt his face reddening again. Harry and Pete, having seen the sign, were doubled over laughing. Avery had seen it too. She gave Sharlee a sad smile and a little wave from the bench.

"A-Ver-Y! A-Ver-Y!" Sharlee began chanting. For a short time, Avery's fan club joined in enthusiastically. But after Avery turned and signaled for them to stop, they did. Sharlee chanted the name by herself a couple more times before settling down at her mother's urging.

The whole thing ate at Derek. He was still thinking about it when, with one out and a man on first after a walk, the hitter smashed a line drive right at him.

If Derek caught it, he knew it would be easy to double up the runner at first base before he could get back safely.

The ball wasn't hit that hard, but it caught him just a little off guard. The ball clanked off the heel of his glove, skittering away and allowing the runners to advance.

It was his first error of the season—and for the third time that day, Derek felt his face go red. Things got even worse when the next hitter doubled in both runners, tying the game back up at three apiece.

Derek felt like slamming his glove on the ground when he got back to the bench at the end of the inning. His error had opened the door for the Red Sox and let in their first run. That, in turn, had led to another pair of runs—and it was *all because of him*!

"Don't worry, Derek—we'll get 'em back."

It was Avery, giving him a confident nod.

Wow, he thought. *She has to just sit there most of the time, but she's still in the game.*

He nodded back, then waved to Sharlee and his folks, who were clapping and shouting, "Go, Yanks!"

The team battled hard. They put two runners on base and got them to second and third, but Pete struck out trying to hit a homer when a measly single would have scored two and tied the game back up.

Things went from bad to worse in the bottom of the second when, with no one out and a runner on third, the batter hit a slow grounder to Pete. The kid on third took off for home. By the time Pete fielded the ball, he had no chance to get him—but he threw home anyway. The runner scored easily.

JJ threw the ball back to Harry—but Harry and Pete were busy yelling at each other, and the ball went out into short center field. By that time, the kid on base had made it all the way to second!

"Da-ad!" Pete whined, looking over at the bench.

Coach K was shaking his head in disgust. Coach Stafford yelled, "Heads in the game!"

"Come on, you guys!" Avery shouted from the bench. "Focus!"

Whoa. Derek was shocked that she'd dared to speak up like that. Not that he blamed her—he felt like doing the same thing.

Ryan started yelling at Pete. Pete yelled back, and

soon they were arguing over whose fault it was that the Sox now had a runner on second. Pete gave Ryan a hard shove, sending him to the ground.

"Hey! Hey!" Coach Stafford and Coach K both ran out there, eager to regain control of the situation.

"Pete, sit down," Coach Stafford told him in no uncertain terms.

"But I'm fine! Really!"

"Pete? Let's go." Coach K took his son's elbow again and led him off the field.

Coach Stafford put his fingers to his mouth and whistled loudly. Then he pointed to the bench. "Mullins! Let's go! You're in for Pete!"

Derek felt a rush of surprise and excitement go through him. He couldn't believe it—maybe Coach *had* been listening to him!

Derek wasn't the only one surprised to see the coach call on the only girl on his roster at a key moment. Both benches were abuzz, and several people in the stands—including Derek's whole family—were standing and clapping. Sharlee held up her sign and jumped up and down.

Avery kept a serious face on, but Derek knew she must have been totally taken by surprise. He hoped she was ready for the challenge and the pressure, because here it was, full force.

As she got to second, Avery pounded her mitt a couple

times, then pointed it at Derek. "Let's do this!" she said, with a fierce look in her eyes.

Derek nodded, but he couldn't suppress a grin. And when he smiled, she allowed herself a brief smile back.

Derek could see that the Red Sox bench was having a laugh riot over Avery getting in the game. He hoped she showed them, big-time.

Harry walked the next batter, putting men on first and second. But he came back to strike out the next man. Then a ground ball that Avery handled cleanly and flipped to first, and it was two out, runners on second and third.

As soon as Avery made the play, a chorus of sarcastic cheers went up from some of the Yankees—applauding her as if she'd made the play of the century, when it had been a pretty easy chance.

"Pipe down, you guys!" Derek yelled before he could think better of it.

"Ooooooh!" Norman and Mark said, their hands over their mouths. Some of the others laughed too, finding it hilarious.

Harry threw his best fastball, and the hitter swung hard, but managed only a weak pop-up to the infield. Avery called it first, but Harry was already racing for it. Seeing him coming, she leaped out of the way just in the nick of time.

But Harry wound up muffing it, and the fifth run scored for the Red Sox.

Harry, Pete, Ryan . . . they're all hogging it out there, Derek thought angrily. *And they're costing us the game!*

That was how he saw it—but obviously, there were some Yankees who were blaming Avery instead. "Go back to softball!" someone shouted. Derek thought it might have been Pete, but he couldn't tell for sure.

The next batter struck out, and mercifully, the Red Sox turn at bat was finally over.

The fourth inning went by without any runs scored. In the Yankees' half of the fifth, Mason struck out, and then Derek lined one hard to short. The shortstop didn't hold on to it, but was able to pick it up and throw him out by a step.

Now Derek was *really* frustrated. That might have been his last at-bat of the day, and he'd come so close to a big hit!

With two out and no one on, Avery came to bat in Pete's spot. It was her first at bat in a while, and Derek wondered if she'd be able to hit this kid's fastball without any warm-up swings.

He needn't have worried. On the first pitch, Avery slugged a screaming liner over the first baseman's head! As the right fielder made the long run to retrieve it, Avery shot off like a bullet. When the dust cleared, she was standing at second base, roaring and smacking her hands together. "LET'S GOOO!!!" she screamed.

Harry was up next. He took two strikes right down the

middle, and the Yankees bench and fans moaned. Next pitch, he swung at one in the dirt and dribbled it right back to the pitcher, who scooped it up and threw Harry out to end the threat.

The bottom of the fifth brought another surprise. "Mullins—I heard you can pitch, is that right?"

"Me?" Avery asked, pointing to herself in surprise.

"You know another Mullins around here?"

"Wow. Uh, yeah—I mean, yes, I can pitch some."

"Well, go pitch some. Harry's reached his pitch limit. Let's see what you've got. Keep 'em right here, and we've still got a chance."

Avery must have felt like she was flying. Derek sure hoped she didn't embarrass herself and ruin her big chance. "Just pretend you're on the Hill with your buddies," he told her, giving her a thumbs-up.

She nodded back. No smiles this time. All business. She warmed up, tossing a few in to JJ. Derek heard the catcher's glove pop with each impact. A murmur of surprise went up from the stands and both benches. Derek had seen her pitch on the Hill, so he wasn't surprised—but obviously, she'd just made an impression on everyone else.

The heart of the Red Sox order was due up to bat. Avery stared in at JJ, wound up, and fired. The hitter finished his swing before the slow change even got there. Strike one!

Avery threw him another one, producing another whiff, although not as embarrassing a miss this time. On the third pitch, with the hitter primed for a third big fat change-up, Avery fired her best fastball right by him for the strikeout!

"Woo! Oh my goodness!" Vijay yelled. Cries of shock and awe went up from the whole Yankees bench. They couldn't believe what they were seeing!

Avery started the next hitter with some other kind of junk ball she'd invented on the Hill, or wherever she'd played before that. He whiffed just like the hitter before him. She threw a fastball next for strike two. The hitter finally managed a weak pop-up to first. Ryan bagged it and threw it around the horn.

Avery blew out a breath and turned to face the next hitter. She went with her fastball first. He swung so hard he nearly came out of his shoes—and hit a weak grounder to Derek, who threw across his body to Ryan for the out. End of inning!

"Easy as one, two, three!" he told Avery, giving her a clap on the back as they jogged back to the bench.

"Let's go get this game!" she told all her teammates as she hit the bench.

The guys were still smiling their knowing smiles, but they gave her high fives this time. "Give it up for the girl!" said Harry.

Derek felt sure the Yankees were going to come back and win the game. For the first time, his teammates had seen what Avery could do to help them win. They were giving her a little support now!

It had to be a huge momentum shift. At least he hoped so. . . .

But no such luck. The Yankees went down 1-2-3 in the sixth to lose the game—going out not with a bang, but with a whimper.

Derek was crestfallen. After all that had happened, here they were, 1–2 in their young season. A losing team again—one where everyone wanted to hog the ball, and no one wanted to pull for one another and play like a team.

Maybe what had happened today would change things going forward. He sure hoped so. Because the season was almost one-third gone already! The Yankees didn't have another game to waste if they wanted to make the playoffs.

"Good game, old man!" his mom said. "You guys almost pulled it off."

"Sorry, Mom."

"Sorry? Sorry for what?"

"I promised you we'd win, and that I'd hit you a homer."

"Aw, don't worry, old man. That's baseball. It's not like you can order up victories and homers."

Derek shook his head dejectedly. "We messed up so bad," he said. "*I* messed up."

"Hey, everyone makes errors," his dad said. "It won't be the last one you make. Just learn from today. You know how to fix it."

Derek nodded. His dad understood him. Derek already

knew what he'd done wrong on that play, way back in the first inning. Next time, he'd look the ball into his glove before turning to throw, and not let himself be distracted.

Derek saw Avery being congratulated by her mom and her friends. She wasn't smiling, any more than he was. They both hated losing. Still, she seemed somehow lighter—less miserable than she usually was around here.

"Hey, look at the bright side, old man," his mom said. "You might have lost this game, but today, your coaches discovered a new player!"

His mom was right, he thought. Now, if only he could get the rest of the team to really accept Avery!

Chapter Thirteen
WHAT'S THE WORD?

"Guess what? We won again!" Sharlee told Derek as the family drove home together, with Vijay sitting in back between Derek and his sister.

"Wow," said Derek. "Cool."

"Aren't you excited, Derek?" she asked, frowning. "We're 4–0—and we're also undefeated!"

"They're the same thing," Derek pointed out.

"Derek," his mom said in a scolding tone.

"That's amazing, Sharlee," Derek said, finally mustering some enthusiasm.

"And I hit a home run! *And* I was the pitcher! But it's different in softball."

"Sharlee, when is your next game?" Vijay asked. "Maybe Derek and I can come."

"Yay!" Sharlee said. "Daddy, when is my next game?"

"Next Saturday," said Mr. Jeter, who was driving. "But I think the boys have a game that morning too."

"Awww," Sharlee groaned, disappointed.

"Don't worry, Sharlee," said Vijay. "We'll find some time to watch you. And you're going to have to hit a home run to show us how you do it."

Derek saw his mom smile at Vijay in the rearview mirror. Everyone loved him—kids, parents, dogs, cats—even mice! Looking at Vijay, Derek thought there had to be something to this optimistic business.

"Can you drop me off at Vijay's?" Derek asked. "We've got to put in some time on our science project."

"*Our* project?" Mrs. Jeter repeated. "I thought you were working with Gary."

Derek winced. "I am. But we needed Vijay's help."

"Derek," said Mr. Jeter. "Aren't you and Gary supposed to do your own work?"

"We *are*!" Derek insisted. "It's just—well, Vijay has the mice we need. Gary's mom wouldn't let him keep them at their house. And I knew *we* weren't going to get them. So . . ."

"Don't worry, Mrs. Jeter," Vijay said. "I am going to be getting extra credit!"

"Oh! Well, in that case . . ."

"Here we are, Vijay," said Mr. Jeter. "Derek, what about lunch?"

"Don't worry, Mr. Jeter," said Vijay, all smiles. "My mom made chapatis and saag paneer. We will be fine."

Derek didn't know what chapatis and saag paneer were, and he was pretty sure his folks didn't either. But one thing they all knew was what a great cook Mrs. Patel was.

Gary was already there, waiting for them. He was in the middle of teaching the mice how to navigate the maze, by using cheese as a reward for learning. Mrs. Patel was in the kitchen, and the smells coming their way made Derek instantly hungry.

The mice seemed hungry too. There were two of them, a large male named Mickey, and a smaller female, of course named Minnie. Gary busily tracked their movements in the maze and counted how many cubes of cheese each one of them found and ate, and how long it took each mouse to find the cheese under different conditions.

Soon Vijay was down on the floor with him, and the two of them were making rapid progress. Derek took notes, registering the data. He had to admit it was fun observing the mice do their thing. He also noted proudly what a good job he'd done building the maze. This project was going to get them all an A-plus, he was sure of it.

After a break for lunch, Derek said, "So where are we at this point?"

Gary and Vijay looked at each other and shrugged. "We have pretty much all we need to make our presentation. But we can always use more data to back up our conclusions."

"Definitely," Vijay agreed. "We should put in at least a few more hours. That way I will be *sure* to get my extra credit!"

When he finally got to the Hill late in the afternoon, Avery and her friends were already there. Derek got in the game, and soon forgot about everything that was troubling him.

There was nothing like a good game of pickup baseball. Everyone was in a good mood, having fun, arguing over whether a ball was fair or foul, or whether someone had missed the rock that was third base on their way around the diamond.

Derek noticed again how free and easy Avery seemed here on the Hill. With the Yankees, she was so grim and serious. Here, she was still intense but also smiled a lot, laughed with her friends, and joked around like every-body else.

A few minutes later, Harry showed up, along with Jeff and two other Hill regulars. There were enough kids now, so nobody had to double up and play for both sides.

And then the familiar black Mercedes showed up, and Dave got out with his mitt and a bat.

"Hey, Derek!" he called, waving and jogging over to the others. "Long time, no play ball!"

"What's up?" Derek said, giving his friend the hand shake they'd made up together. "Haven't seen much of you the past couple weeks."

"Well, you know," Dave said with a grin. "Got to get my golf game in gear."

Dave's dream was to be a professional golfer on the PGA Tour. He and Derek had bonded over their lofty ambitions and had been close friends ever since. In fact, if Derek had to choose Dave or Vijay as his best friend, he would have had a really hard time deciding.

"How'd your team do yesterday?" Derek asked him.

"We won again, 10–2. That makes us 3–0. Chase is a great coach, and he learned a lot from your dad last year, too."

"Cool. That's great, man."

"How's your team doing?"

"We're 1–2," Derek said.

"Oh. Well, hey, it's still early. You guys will get it turned around."

"I hope."

"Not next game, though," Dave said with a grin. "It's you against us."

"Hey, Derek!" Avery called from second base. "You playing or not?"

"Oh," said Dave, realizing that the second baseman was a girl. "Sorry. Go ahead. We'll talk after the inning's over."

"No, man, it's okay. What were you saying?"

"Derek!" Avery called impatiently.

"Sorry. Hang out a few minutes, okay? Talk to you after this inning."

Derek proceeded to fly out to center. While the rest of his team continued their at bats, he went back over to talk to his friend.

Dave looked over at Avery. "So . . . that's her, huh?"

"Who?"

"Avery."

"Oh. Yeah. She's on my team. The Yankees, I mean."

"Right. I heard." Dave seemed suddenly uncomfortable.

"What?" Derek asked. "What's the matter?"

"Oh, nothing," Dave said quickly, avoiding Derek's gaze. "I didn't realize you were here with her, that's all."

"I'm not 'here with her,'" Derek corrected him. "I'm just *here*, like always. These other kids are all here because their field is being renovated over on the south side."

"Oh. Okay."

"No, seriously."

"I *said* okay!"

"What *exactly* did you hear about Avery?"

"Well . . . that you guys . . . I don't know . . . *like* each other and stuff."

"WHAT? No way!"

"Ah, you know how people make stuff up. They said you guys were hanging out. And that someone asked her if she liked you, and she said 'Sure—who doesn't like Derek Jeter?'"

"Wait a minute!" Derek said, holding up a hand. "That

doesn't mean she *likes* me. She said, 'Who doesn't?'! As in, 'He's a nice kid'!"

"Okay. If you say so.*"*

"I *do* say so!" Derek shook his head, then calmed himself down. "Look, I'm not mad at *you*. But I hate when people start making stuff up."

"I hear you. Anyway, that got around, and then the kids from the Yankees were talking about how you're always sticking up for her, and someone saw you walking her home one time. . . ."

Uh-oh. This was bad. *Very* bad.

It was one thing for clowns like Elliott and Norman and Pete and Harry to make jokes about his friendship with Avery. But if *Dave* was already hearing about it, the rumor mill had clearly gotten way out of hand.

It almost made him want to stay far away from Avery altogether. But he quickly rejected that idea.

"Look, I'm really sorry, Derek," Dave said. "I didn't mean to upset you or anything. But that's what people are saying."

"We're just friends, okay? I'm totally serious, man. And you can tell everyone else that—straight from the horse's mouth."

"You got it," Dave promised.

"Hey, Derek!" Avery said, coming up behind them. "You still in the game?"

"Uh, yeah!"

"Well, get out there, then!"

He ran out to play short, but his head was a million miles away.

Meeting Avery had taught him that girls and boys *could* be friends.

He was pretty sure he'd convinced Dave, at least. But Dave was one of his best friends and could be counted on to be in his corner.

As for all the other kids who "happened to hear" about him and Avery? Well, he didn't have to let any of that get to him, did he? At least he knew his close friends and his family would stick up for him, no matter what anybody said.

Chapter Fourteen
THE WORM TURNS

Friday was the first day of science project demonstrations. Vijay and Sheila's project went first. Derek noticed how Sheila gave most of the presentation—which was about an electromagnetic contraption they'd built—while Vijay only talked a little.

Too bad, thought Derek. Vijay was a really good story-teller. Sheila, not so much. She droned on until Ms. Terrapin told her to wrap it up, as they had many more projects to get to that day.

After a few more presentations, which were fairly dull, it was time for them to present their work!

Gary had agreed to do the presentation, with Vijay handling the mice and Derek pointing to charts and graphs to illustrate Gary's points. That was fine with Derek. He had never been fond of public speaking, preferring to let other people do most of the talking.

Things went well at first. The class perked up as soon as Gary informed them that mice in a maze were the subject of the experiment. They got up from their desks and crowded around to see—except for some kids who hung back out of sheer terror of rodents.

The cute little white mice skittered all over Vijay's arms as he put them gently down inside Derek's intricate maze, and Gary began demonstrating.

The mice, Mickey and Minnie, had learned their lessons well. But when Gary moved the cheese to a different spot in the maze, they had to learn all over again. How quickly would they do it? The class was spellbound, watching the experiment repeat itself in real time.

Things began to go wrong when Gary tripped over the base of the stand that was holding the charts. He tumbled backward, hitting the maze, and breaking one of its cardboard walls.

Terrified, Mickey and Minnie headed straight for the gap, escaping the confines of the maze before Vijay or anyone else could catch them!

Panic was in full bloom. Kids were standing on chairs, and more than a few of them were shrieking in terror.

The mice, frightened by the noise and stomping feet, went crazy running all over the room, while poor Vijay called out their names, trying in vain to rescue his tiny pets.

Luckily, Derek was in the right place at the right time, and grabbed Minnie with both hands and put her back in the cage. As he did, Mickey came scurrying right over to Derek, seeing his pal Minnie safe in their little home away from home.

The panic and noise gradually subsided, just in time for the bell signaling the end of the school day.

"Gary, Vijay, and Derek," Ms. Terrapin called out. "Please stay for a moment. I want to speak to you privately."

Uh-oh. Derek was sure this could not be good news.

But he was surprised when Ms. Terrapin told the three of them, "I'm giving you an A for your project, boys. The written report was top-notch, and the demonstration was fascinating."

She cleared her throat. "It would have been an A-plus, except that you allowed your demonstration to create such a commotion. The next time you bring live animals into class, you'll have to take better care of them. Understood?"

"Yes, Ms. Terrapin," all three boys said together.

As soon as they were out of there, they all looked at one another, wide-eyed.

"Yessss!" Vijay said. "Can you believe it?"

"I thought we were finished," Derek said.

"Dead meat!" Vijay agreed.

"I told you the mouse maze was a great idea," Gary said. "If you hadn't put the stand right in my way, Jeter, there would have been no problem."

"Hey, Gary, every star needs a good supporting cast. Right, Vijay?"

"Definitely!" Vijay agreed, throwing his arm around Derek's shoulder.

"Blah, blah, blah," Gary said, waving a hand in dismissal.

Derek shook his head. As usual, Gary was taking credit for whatever good happened and blaming everyone else for whatever went wrong.

Derek didn't care, though. He was *free*! No more after-school meetings with Gary! No more listening to him run his mouth. And even though Gary had cast himself as the star of the show, Derek knew they wouldn't have gotten an A if they hadn't all worked together. They had different strengths but the same end goal, so ultimately they each played a supporting role.

On Friday night, Derek's mom announced to the family that her boss had called her in to his office and offered her a raise. "It's not a promotion—and it's not what I would have made if I'd *gotten* the promotion—but it's better than nothing for sure," she pronounced.

"That's great, Dot!" Mr. Jeter said, giving his wife a big hug.

"Mommy, how much are they giving you?" Sharlee wanted to know.

"Hey," Mrs. Jeter said, pretending to scold her, "that's privileged information."

"A thousand? A million?"

"Sharlee," said Mr. Jeter.

"You deserve it, Mom," said Derek, hugging her from the other side so that they were all a big sandwich.

"Well, the best part is *how* it happened," said Mrs. Jeter. "The boss told me five separate people had pulled him aside to tell him he should have given me the promotion. He even apologized, saying if he'd known how highly the rest of the staff thought of me, he *would* have. He said the raise was the least he could do, and that he wished it could be more."

"Hmm," said Mr. Jeter skeptically.

"Never mind, Jeter," she told him. "It means a lot to me that my colleagues stood up for me."

Derek's mom was there for his next game, but his dad and Sharlee had their own game at the same hour. So, Mrs. Jeter sat next to Avery's mom and introduced herself.

It occurred to Derek, watching from the field, that he himself had never actually met Avery's mom. She looked like an athlete, he observed, remembering that she had been a sports pioneer back in the day. Avery's two older friends Max and Roger were there as well.

Derek, Vijay, and Avery had been the first three kids

to show up. They'd immediately started tossing a ball around.

After a few minutes, more kids started showing up. Derek wanted to play some catch with the others, too. People were already talking about him and Avery, and he didn't want to give them any new ammunition.

On the other hand, he suddenly thought, what did he care what stupid stuff people thought or said or made up? Why *should* he care? The people who had his back—his family, Vijay, Dave—*they* were the ones who counted most.

The black Mercedes pulled up to the curb, and out jumped Dave. He dragged a duffel bag out of the trunk and carried it to the opposite bench. The Tigers had arrived.

Derek knew a few of them, so he walked over to say hi. He shook hands with Chase, who said, "Good to see you again, Derek—it's been a while."

"You too, sir."

"Wish we had you on our team, but that's how it goes, huh? How're you guys doing?"

Derek moved his head from side to side. "Ah, you know . . . so-so."

"Hmmm." Chase gave him a penetrating look. "Every-thing okay?"

Derek thought for a moment, then nodded. "I think so. I think it will be, anyway. Thanks."

"Well, let's make it a good game today, huh?"

"You bet!"

Derek went over to Dave, and they did their handshake, just like old times.

"It's weird to see you in that uniform," Dave said, grinning. "You've always wanted to wear it."

Dave knew all about Derek's dreams. They'd spent lots of time talking about the future. Which made Derek realize how little time they'd been spending together since basketball season ended.

Being on the same team mattered, it turned out. But Dave was one of his best friends, no matter what.

"Hey, now that science projects are over, you want to come over and play ball on the Hill?" Derek asked him.

"Sure," Dave said. "I was just kind of hanging back, 'cause I heard . . . you know . . . So sure, we'll make it happen, soon. Oh yeah—and if you want, we can do a round of golf together a week from Sunday."

"I'll check with my folks. Anyway, have a good one."

"You too."

They didn't wish each other good luck, of course. Just to "have a good game." Golf might have been Dave's main focus, but he was a competitor, just like Derek. And like Avery, too.

After infield practice, Coach Stafford gathered the team together in a circle. "Sit down," he told them. "Make yourselves comfortable. I've got something I want to say to all of you. Something I've been thinking about for a while, and particularly since our last game."

A murmur went around the circle, and kids furtively glanced at one another.

"We're a talented team," he said, "but we're losing games to teams we should beat. Do you want to know why? Because everyone on this team wants to be the big star. Well, let me ask you all—who here ever saw a movie where everyone was the star?"

No one had.

"Now, baseball's a funny game. There are teams, sure—but at any given moment, it's just one person, starring with a bat, or a mitt, or a ball. Everyone else has to *support* that person—be ready to take a relay, or back up a throw, or make that tag.

"And they have to be *thinking* like a team! We need to get our heads in the game—and that means no making fun of one another. No sniggers behind people's backs. No hogging other people's plays.

"Any great movie has a great supporting cast," he concluded. "And a great supporting cast *supports one another*." He looked slowly at each of them in turn. "And that means every single one of you."

For a few seconds, there was a deep silence. Then Avery spoke up.

"Coach? Can I say something?"

Coach Stafford seemed startled, but he nodded. "Sure."

"I know my being here bothers some of you guys—but that's too bad. I'm here because I *want* to be here. I love this game as much as any of you, and I'm not going away anytime soon. We're supposed to be on the same side. So, let's play against the other team instead of ourselves, okay?"

"You heard it, Yankees!" the coach said. "All right. Anybody else? No? Okay, then. I've said what I have to say. Now go out there and let's win this game—*as a team!*"

Chapter Fifteen
SEEDS OF HOPE

The Yankees took the field first. And for the first time all season, Avery was in the starting lineup. There she stood, behind Derek in left field. Derek touched his cap in salutation, and she nodded back, pounding her mitt with her fist and jumping up and down on the balls of her feet.

Derek scanned the rest of the field. Mason was out in center as usual, and Vijay was in right.

Derek remembered when his friend had been strictly a sub. But years of playing ball all the time with Derek, and being coached by Derek's dad, had made Vijay a much better ballplayer.

Tre' was at third, Pete at second, and Ryan at first. JJ was catching, and Harry was on the mound.

Derek looked over at the Yankees bench. Norman, Mark, Miles, and Elliott were all there. But something was different. None of them were goofing around, trying to make one another laugh. They were all standing, leaning against the chain-link fence, and cheering the team on.

Obviously, Coach Stafford's talk had a big effect.

"Play ball!" cried the ump.

Derek tossed in the ball they'd been using for infield practice and got into "ready" position.

The Tigers' roster was loaded. Derek knew Dave, Chris Chang, and Tyrone Murray, all former teammates, and all pretty good. There were a few others he didn't know but recognized from past years. Good athletes, all of them—and several looked big and strong enough to hit home runs.

Harry was going to have his work cut out for him for sure. And the Yankees were going to have to do some serious scoring if they wanted to keep up.

The first hitter started out by trying to hit the ball to the next county. Harry seemed to sense his overeagerness and went to a changeup. The kid was way out in front and popped up to Ryan at first.

The next player up was more patient. He let Harry throw five pitches, running the count full—then grooved a fastball that sailed over Derek's head. He turned and saw Avery running after it, glove extended. She managed to knock it down so it didn't get past her—which surely would have resulted in a home run.

"Second base!" Derek yelled, seeing that the runner was trying to stretch it into a double. He ran to cover the bag.

Avery heard him, picked up the ball, and fired a strike on one hop. Derek snagged it and put the tag on the runner's helmet.

"Out!" yelled the ump.

"WOO-HOO!"

The cheer went up from the Yankees' bench, and the stands on their side of the field. Derek turned to Avery and clapped his hand and his mitt together, applauding the play. She pointed back at him.

Dave came to the plate, and Derek got deeper into his crouch. He knew his friend was a pull hitter with lots of power, and could hit a line drive anywhere, anytime.

Sure enough, Dave laced one right at Tre', who had to cover his face to avoid getting creamed by the ball. It ricocheted off his mitt, heading Derek's way.

Derek took two steps, picked up the ball, and fired toward first without even looking.

"Out!" the umpire called, and another big cheer went up from the home side of the field.

Inning over!

The Tigers' starting pitcher was a real fireballer. Derek watched as he threw his warm-ups. The catcher's mitt sounded with an explosive pop on every pitch.

That must hurt, Derek couldn't help thinking. He

wondered how many of his teammates would be able to get around on that fastball.

Mason, the Yankees' leadoff man, was a good contact hitter who didn't try to do too much. Sure enough, he managed to slap a single between first and second.

Up came Derek. He dug in to the batter's box, but he had to duck and dive away from the first pitch, which came right at his head!

After that, he couldn't help being a little wary. He took the next one right down the middle for strike one. Then he looked down at Coach K, who was acting as third base coach—and the coach gave him the bunt sign!

Derek didn't like it. He was sure he could hit this pitcher's best fastball, given two more strikes. But it wasn't his decision—and he remembered Coach Stafford's words. This wasn't about him being a hero or a star. It was about everybody being part of the supporting cast.

He got into bunting position, "catching the ball with the bat," as his dad had taught him. The ball rolled right down the line. The third baseman was waiting for it and threw Derek out at first.

But now, Mason was at second. And the bunt paid off when he got to third on a wild pitch, and Pete then lifted a sacrifice fly to center for the game's first run.

Harry struck out, and so did JJ. But at least they'd touched up the Tigers for a run, and the early lead!

It didn't hold up long, though. Harry was a good pitcher,

and he wasn't walking anyone, but the Tigers were good hitters. Some of them hit it right at the defense. But others found holes. Strong play by the Yankees fielders prevented what might have been much worse damage. Still, by the middle of the third inning, it was 3–1, Tigers.

Avery led off the Yankee half of the inning. She was batting ninth in the order, but if that bothered her, she didn't show it.

She got into the batter's box and waggled the bat around over her shoulder. The Tigers pitcher walked off the mound for a second and said something to the shortstop and third baseman that made them all laugh.

Derek thought he knew what they were joking about—and he was sure Avery did too. If he were her, it would have made him mad—and that might have made him overswing.

But Avery did *not* overswing. She kept her balance, and let the speed of the pitch provide the power as the ball ricocheted off her bat and sailed over the right fielder's head.

By the time he got to it and threw it back in, Avery was sliding into third base with a clean leadoff triple! Now it was Mason's turn to sacrifice. The squeeze play worked, with Avery barreling home. Mason was out at first, but the run scored to narrow the gap to 3–2.

Then Derek stepped up to the plate. He copied Avery's approach. *Just swing level . . . keep the bat in the hitting zone and slap it right back through the middle. . . .*

It worked. Derek drilled a line drive that made the pitcher duck and cover. The ball skittered over second base for a single.

Pete came to the plate next. Chase went out to visit the mound to calm his pitcher down. Whatever he said, the pitcher seemed to recover, striking Pete out on three fastballs.

But Derek had been watching the pitcher's windup, and noticed it was pretty slow.

On the second strike to Harry, Derek took off for third!

The catcher threw—wildly. The ball hit Derek's cleat and bounced into left field. Derek then got up and scampered home for the tying run!

Now the pitcher was *really* rattled. He threw a screaming fastball that hit Harry square in his pitching arm!

Harry went down with a cry of pain, gripping his bicep and rolling on the ground. Coach Stafford and Coach K ran over to him, checking the severity of the injury. After a while, Harry got up and, flexing his arm, made his way slowly to first base.

Derek guessed the arm wasn't broken, or they would have taken Harry out right away. But he wondered whether Harry would be able to keep pitching—especially if the arm started swelling up and throbbing.

JJ came to the plate, as focused as the Tiger pitcher was rattled. He creamed the first pitch between the center fielder and right fielder for a home run! Harry yelled in triumph, holding up his good arm, while the one that had been hit hung at his side.

Chase came out and made a pitching substitution. The new pitcher didn't throw nearly as hard as the first, but he managed to strike Ryan out, swinging at ball four.

"Avery!" Coach Stafford said. "You're pitching. Get out there and warm up with JJ!"

Avery couldn't throw as hard as Harry, true, thought Derek—but that didn't mean she couldn't get guys out, did it?

The Tigers must have been falling all over each other to get to the plate, he guessed. *Facing a girl on the mound? Where's my bat?!*

But Avery was wise to them, it turned out. She fed them a tricky variety of slow stuff, changing her delivery with every pitch. One would come in side-arm, another over the top, and after that, a quick pitch with hardly any windup.

Two Tigers in a row went down swinging.

After her quick start, though, Avery seemed to lose the plate. The hitters, getting the idea now, lay off her slow stuff, and worked two straight walks.

Then Dave came up. Unlike the others, he'd seen Avery play on the Hill that day, and knew enough to take her seriously. He was patient, watched a few pitches go by, then laced a long fly to left! It landed behind Miles, who raced after it as Dave barreled around the bases.

Already the two runners ahead of him had scored. Dave

was going to end up with an easy triple, Derek thought, as he got into position to receive the throw from Miles. With the throw in the air, a roar went up from the assembled crowd. Derek knew what that meant without turning to look—Dave was trying to stretch his triple into a home run!

Derek caught the ball, wheeled, and fired a bullet in the general direction of home plate.

He hadn't had the chance to aim. Rather, he'd relied on instinct and years of practice. His throw got there just in time, and JJ nailed Dave for the out to end the inning!

The Yankees were playing their best ball of the season by far, but they were behind now, 5–4. Tre' popped up, Vijay grounded out, and Avery was robbed of a double by a great play at third, with Dave laying out to catch the line drive a few inches off the ground.

Six pitches and the Yankees were done, and Avery was right back on the mound.

The Tigers had adjusted to her by now, and she wasn't fooling anybody. Still, she managed—with some good fielding behind her—to get through the inning without yielding any more runs. The Tigers stranded men on second and third. To Derek, that was a good sign.

The Yankees' fifth began with Mason striking out. That meant it was up to Derek to get the rally going. He knew this would probably be his last at bat of the game, and he was determined to make it count.

Seeing that the third baseman was playing him deep,

Derek decided to try to bunt for a base hit. He laid one down, right on the third-base line, and sped toward first. As he got there, he watched the catcher's throw sail over the first baseman's head. Derek headed for second, clapping his hands when he got there and yelling, "Let's go!"

Pete came up to bat, and Derek started to worry. Of all the kids on the team, Pete was usually the one to try to be a hero, swinging for the fences, when all they needed now was a single to tie the game back up.

But Pete must have been listening to the coach's speech, too—because he held off on two straight pitches just off the strike zone. And when he got his pitch, he took it to the opposite field. Derek scampered around third and slid into home just ahead of the relay throw.

Tie game!

Miles came up. It would have been Harry, but Harry was sitting on the bench with an ice pack wrapped around his sore arm. It didn't seem to be distracting him from cheering for the team, though, Derek noticed. Much to his satisfaction, the Yankees seemed finally to be playing like a real team.

Miles struck out on three pitches, and JJ followed with a sharp grounder that caught Pete off-guard, halfway between second and third. He wound up caught in a rundown, a sure out. But he had the sense to get tagged out sliding into third, so that JJ could sneak into second behind him.

With two outs, it was all up to Ryan. He kept fouling off pitch after pitch with two strikes, until the pitcher finally made a mistake and left one where he could hit it. Ryan punched it into center field, and Pete scored the go-ahead run!

Tre' struck out to end the fifth, but now, the Yankees had the Tigers by the tail, down to their last licks. If Avery could hold them off, the Yankees would have their biggest win of the season.

Avery was tired now, Derek could tell. Her control wasn't as good, and she walked two batters in a row after getting the first out. The next hitter looped a fly ball behind third base.

Derek couldn't tell if it was foul or fair, but he knew if he caught it, it was another out. He dove, turning his glove upward as he fell—and came up with the ball!

The runners both tagged up before he could get up and throw it back in, so now there were men at second and third—but there were also two outs.

One more, Avery . . . just one more . . . !

The hitter swung. The ball went high and far, to right center field. The runners took off for home, as Vijay ran to make the play.

"I got it! I got it!" he shouted. But just before he got to it, he caught his cleat in the grass and fell to the ground. Derek gasped, along with everyone else there.

The ball hit off Vijay's cleat, and bounded back into the

air. It came down right on top of him. Vijay—lying on his back—grabbed it with two hands for the final out of the game!

"YESSSSSS!! WOO-HOO!!"

Half the crowd cheered, the other half moaned, and the ballgame was over. Yankees 6, Tigers 5!

The whole team ran to the mound and formed a circle of hugging, jumping, screaming winners. *A team, at last*, Derek thought happily.

"What a game!" Vijay exulted, hugging Derek, Avery, and everyone else he could get his arms around. "What an awesome game!"

Derek had to agree. It had been a long time since he'd felt this way about his baseball team—more than a year, in fact.

No one Yankee had been responsible for the victory— they'd *all* contributed, both physically and emotionally. Every one of them had a hand in this win. They were *all* a supporting cast, thought Derek.

If they could keep it up for the rest of the season, they had every reason to think they could make the playoffs. *Even with a girl on the team*, he thought with a wry grin.

There was still a long way to go, he knew. But if they could play this way once, they could do it again. It meant they'd gotten past having a girl on the team. Now, they were only *Yankees*.

Avery came up to Derek and Vijay, smiling. Guys were

patting her on the back and telling her, "Great game!" And she seemed to be enjoying herself for the first time.

"Thanks, Vijay," she said. "I mean it. Thanks. Really."

"For what?" Vijay asked innocently.

"For standing up for me. From the get-go."

"Why wouldn't I?" said Vijay. Then he turned to accept high fives from the other kids for his fantastic, game-ending catch.

"You too, Derek."

"Aw, it was nothing," Derek said.

But he knew, and so did she, that it hadn't been easy getting to this point—and that it probably wouldn't be the last time they'd have to deal with dumb stuff.

Still, she was their *friend* now, and nothing anyone said or did was going to change that.

"Your brother would have been proud of you today," he told her.

She pressed her lips together hard and nodded. "Thanks," she said. "Thanks for that."

Then she went off to hug Max, Roger, and her mom. As Derek watched her, he thought, *A person has to have a good supporting cast.*

And he had one, in spades. Between his parents, sister, grandparents, aunts, uncles, and cousins, and his friends Vijay, Dave—and Avery—he couldn't have asked for more.

JETER PUBLISHING

Jeter Publishing's seventh middle-grade book is inspired by the childhood of Derek Jeter, who grew up playing baseball. The middle-grade series is based on the principles of Jeter's Turn 2 Foundation.

Jeter Publishing encompasses adult nonfiction, children's picture books, middle-grade fiction, ready-to-read children's books, and children's nonfiction.

JETER'S LEADERS

is a leadership development program created to empower, recognize, and enhance the skills of high school students who:

- **PROMOTE HEALTHY LIFESTYLES AND ARE FREE OF ALCOHOL AND SUBSTANCE ABUSE**

- **ACHIEVE ACADEMICALLY**

- **ARE COMMITTED TO IMPROVING THEIR COMMUNITY THROUGH SOCIAL CHANGE ACTIVITIES**

- **SERVE AS ROLE MODELS TO YOUNGER STUDENTS AND DELIVER POSITIVE MESSAGES TO THEIR PEERS**

Photo credit: Eileen Barroso/Turn 2 Foundation, Inc.

> "Your role models should teach you, inspire you, criticize you, and give you structure. My parents did all of these things with their contracts. They tackled every subject. There was nothing we didn't discuss. I didn't love every aspect of it, but I was mature enough to understand that almost everything they talked about made sense." **—DEREK JETER**

DO YOU HAVE WHAT IT TAKES TO BECOME A
JETER'S LEADER?

- I am drug and alcohol free.
- I volunteer in my community.
- I am good to the environment.
- I am a role model for kids.
- I do not use the word "can't."
- I am a role model for my peers and younger kids.
- I stand up for what's right.

- I am respectful to others.
- I encourage others to participate.
- I am open-minded.
- I set my goals high.
- I do well in school.
- I like to exercise and eat well to keep my body strong.
- I am educated on current events.

CREATE A CONTRACT

What are your goals?

Sit down with your parents or an adult mentor to create your own contract to help you take the first step toward achieving your dreams.

For more information on JETER'S LEADERS, visit
TURN2FOUNDATION.ORG

About the Authors

DEREK JETER played Major League Baseball for the New York Yankees for twenty seasons and is a five-time World Series champion. He is a true legend in professional sports and a role model for young people on and off the field and through his work in the community with his Turn 2 Foundation. For more information, visit Turn2Foundation.org.

Derek was born in New Jersey and moved to Kalamazoo, Michigan, when he was four. There he often attended Detroit Tigers games with his family, but the New York Yankees were always his favorite team, and he never stopped dreaming of playing for them.

PAUL MANTELL is the author of more than one hundred books for young readers.

BULLYING.
BE A LEADER AND STOP IT.

Do your part to stop bullies in their tracks.

Protect yourself and your friends with STOPit. It's easy. It's anonymous. It's the right thing to do.

"Never let a bully win." - Derek Jeter

Download the app today!

TURN 2 FOUNDATION, INC.

STOP!T